To Don

Elizabeth Foskett

THE OXFORD CONNECTION

AUSTIN MACAULEY PUBLISHERS

LONDON * CAMBRIDGE * NEW YORK * SHARJAH

A CIP catalogue record for this title is available from the British Library.

ISBN 9781035875139 (Paperback)
ISBN 9781035875146 (Hardback)
ISBN 9781035875153 (ePub e-book)

www.austinmacauley.com

First Published 2024
Austin Macauley Publishers Ltd®
1 Canada Square
Canary Wharf
London
E14 5AA

Prologue
Berlin

It was reported in the Berliner Tageszeit that a woman's body, as yet unidentified, was found yesterday in a remote part of the Grunewald on the outskirts of Berlin. She had a single bullet wound in the temple, and a small silver pistol was found at the scene. A police spokesman stated that they are not treating her death as suspicious.

All efforts are being made to identify the body so that the next-of-kin can be informed.

Chapter 1

If Nicholas Stowkovsky had known, when he first set eyes on Heike, the misery she'd leave behind her, would he have married her? It seemed inconceivable that he was even considering this, but over recent months following her inexplicable disappearance, he'd started questioning their relationship. He hated himself for thinking like this because he loved her still and missed her desperately, but lately, these doubts had started creeping into his mind at unexpected moments. This morning, as he woke up yet again in the grey, misty half-light of early dawn, he half-stretched out his arm instinctively to caress her warm body before he remembered how useless it was.

He thrust the duvet impatiently into a crumpled heap and padded over to the window. *Another dreadful night*, he thought as he stared bleakly out at the familiar view. His nightmares were becoming more frequent and always followed the same pattern. Last night had been particularly vivid. There were these familiar figures he was trying vainly to reach—he wasn't sure if it was his wife or his father who was screaming out for his help—but he knew they were both in terrible danger. Their hands were extended towards him, and it was imperative to rescue them. But although he fought valiantly against the inertia of sleep, his limbs obstinately refused to obey him. Their screams were echoing in his ears, and woke up to the sound of a screech owl on a tree close by.

As he stood by the window, these images still lingered. Closing his eyes briefly, he tried to blot them out. The owl called again, further away this time. A glimmer of light in the sky over the peaceful, sleeping village suggested that dawn was approaching. He shivered in the cool October air and shut the window. Leaning on the windowsill, he stood for a moment, staring unseeingly at the quiet lane that passed his front gate. It led out of the little village of Cumnor and then climbed steadily up to the duel carriageway that wound its way down to the city of Oxford some five miles away.

He'd been frantic with worry when Heike hadn't returned to Oxford as expected after three months. Her letters had become fewer, and there had been virtually no phone calls. He realised her line was probably tapped, but in an emergency, he'd have expected some news. Their angry recriminations before she'd left Oxford had left a bitter aftertaste; perhaps, her parents had been right, after all. He'd been aware of their unease about his marriage to Heike. With a tired sigh, he turned away and glanced across the bedroom. If only he could see Heike lying in that large, comfortable bed they had shared for so many years, her red curls a bright splash of colour against the pillow.

"Heike"—the sound of his voice echoed round the quiet room, but saying her name wasn't going to bring her back. Mentally, he tried to shake himself out of these depressing thoughts. It was pointless revisiting all of this and it was getting him nowhere. He squinted at his watch. It was coming up to six-thirty. He was now too wide awake to go back to bed, and he knew that he had a very full day ahead of him. The opening week of the Michaelmas term and a new university year was always a time of frenzied activity, with a fresh intake of excited and nervous students coming up to Oxford for the first time. Nicholas deliberately filled his mind, planning his day while he showered—anything rather than recall that wretched nightmare.

He made a mental check list: another look at those student files, check over all their details and go through the day's programme to firm up all the timings, see the Dean. He ticked them all off methodically as the powerful jets of icy water sprayed over his body, still lean and taut as that of a young man. His wife had joked that the habits of his spartan, Russian childhood had never left him. He resolutely tried to put all thoughts of Heike to the back of his mind; the memories were too bittersweet. His body ached for hers. They had often made love in the shower, he remembered with a stab of pain. He would carry her laughing and protesting from their bedroom and turn the water full on. As they washed and caressed each other, Heike's face turned up to his in mute longing, and all pretence of showering was gone as they clung together, each knowing how to give the other the greatest pleasure.

"What a selfish brute I've been," he muttered aloud, savagely turning off the shower and almost wrenching it from the wall in his frustration. As each day passed, he was beginning to realise how he'd taken her unselfish love for granted. She'd always seemed able to find time to listen patiently to his worries, he remembered bitterly, and he knew that the ever-loyal support she had given him over the years had helped him get where he was now.

Nicholas Stowkovsky had worked long and hard for his professorship and was focussed as only those with a constant, burning ambition would understand. He was highly respected by his colleagues for his drive and determination to extract only the best from his students. Those in his tutorial group knew only too well that he was not a man to be trifled with, and they feared, respected and revered him in equal measure. The female students all fancied him, but Nicholas, long used to young, susceptible girls, met their nervous attempts at flirtation with a half-smile and briskly brushed them aside. That anguish and uncertainty lay behind his assured, autocratic manner would never have entered their minds. Those who worked with him recognised that his mercurial temperament and quick temper often stemmed from an inability to suffer fools gladly or gently. Of late, this temper had become more and more evident. Only friends close to him glimpsed a very private individual and understood the inner torment of his troubled past and its link with his missing wife. His colleagues, though naturally sympathetic about his worries, grumbled to each other that he was becoming increasingly difficult as the months passed.

Nicholas was no fool. He recognised how he had changed over the last couple of years. Though he had, for a while, managed to find comfort in his work, this no longer seemed enough. He was frowning as he rustled through his papers on a desk piled high with books and hastily scribbled notes. He should have been eagerly anticipating this new academic year, but he somehow just could not find the enthusiasm he once had. Over the last couple of years, without Heike, his life seemed to have lost its meaning, and today, he even resented the attention that these new students would need. He had planned a sabbatical for the next nine months, feeling he had to get away for a while, perhaps even travel over to Germany again, however fruitless the continuing search for his wife might seem. Unfortunately, the colleague due to take over from him had had a climbing accident.

"Damn the bloody woman," he said savagely as he searched for a vital folder. "Why did she have to choose this moment to break her leg?"

He found the missing file pushed to the back of an overflowing drawer. As he glanced again at all their personal details, he saw the usual mix of students—mainly young, judging by their photos, but there were one or two more mature. He paused over one, merely noting the name, Maggie Stewart, before pushing it aside. The grainy picture revealed little.

"Another middle-aged woman bored with her life," he assumed with little interest. "Her poor husband's been abandoned so that she can follow some sort of dream, I suppose."

With a sigh, he impatiently thrust his papers into his briefcase and glanced at his watch—almost eight o'clock. There wasn't even time for a quick breakfast if he wanted to pick up the only early-morning bus into Oxford. He grabbed his coat and briefcase and, slamming the front door, hurried down the moss-covered path. The front garden of the little thatched cottage where he and Heike had lived for so many years looked neglected and uncared for. Nicholas didn't have much time or inclination for gardening, therefore this area had become Heike's special joy, and she had spent many hours planting and weeding, so that it was alive with colour throughout the year. Now it looked sad and unkempt.

"Damn it all," he swore again angrily as he tugged impatiently at the stubborn latch of the little gate. It needed fixing and painting. This was yet another task that Heike would have undertaken.

"Morning, Prof," said the postman cheerily as he passed Nicholas on the way to the bus stop. "Do you want to take these with you?" He took a bundle of letters out of his bag.

"Might as well; thanks, Joe," he said, forcing a smile as he took them. At that moment, the bus lumbered round the corner. He was still some distance from the bus stop, and he waved the letters frantically to catch the driver's eye. He nodded briefly to one or two familiar faces and made his way with difficulty down the gangway to the one remaining seat at the back, almost losing letters and briefcase as the bus set off again, lurching round yet another bend. The picturesque village of Cumnor, lying only a few miles from Oxford, was served by just two buses a day, and this local bus was crowded as always. Though many of the old farming cottages had been renovated and were now largely occupied by those working in Oxford, Cumnor still retained a traditional village atmosphere with the usual mix of church, pub, general store and post office. The rich farmland that encircled it ensured its safety from creeping development, and its inhabitants were determined to keep it that way.

It was not until the little bus reached the outskirts of the city that he idly glanced through the bundle of letters still clasped in his hand. Most were business and could wait until later. There was also one from his sister, and his angular features softened at the sight of the long sloping handwriting. He was about to open it when he suddenly glimpsed the envelope underneath with a distinctive

German stamp. His heart seemed to stop. White as a sheet, he ripped it open. Could it be from Heike at last? His trembling fingers had difficulty extracting the single sheet of paper. The words seemed to dance in front of his eyes, and he blinked several times before the printed letters came into focus.

YOU ARE WASTING YOUR TIME LOOKING FOR YOUR WIFE. SHE IS LONG SINCE DEAD. SHE MET A FITTING END FOR A STASI SYMPATHISER.

"Are you alright there, sir?" The driver's concerned face loomed above him, and Nicholas realised with a start that the bus, now empty of passengers, was stationary at the Terminal.

He struggled for some vestige of self-control. "Yes, yes, thank you, just some unexpected news."

He accomplished the walk from the bus station like a sleepwalker, neither noticing nor acknowledging greetings from colleagues as he made his way across the grassy quadrangle and up the steep, winding stairs that led to the blessed privacy of his own rooms.

"Really, Nicholas is becoming impossible these days," grumbled the Dean as she snatched a quick coffee. "He cut me completely dead this morning."

Meanwhile, Nicholas sat in a daze, reading and rereading the few curt words that, if true, raised for him the spectre of his wife as a spy and destroyed his last vestige of hope that he would ever find her alive.

Chapter 2

Three figures sat hunched round the old oak table, the man leaning forward and jabbing his finger on the roughened surface as if to emphasise the points he was making. The two women sat in silence, the younger one nodding in agreement from time to time. Despite the early evening sunshine, the curtains were tightly closed to keep out inquisitive, prying eyes. An elderly lady sat knitting in a rocking chair near the fireplace. The needles clattered nervously as her fingers trembled and fumbled. She kept glancing over at the three young people who seemed oblivious to her presence until the man glanced irritably in her direction.

"Can't you stop that clicking? It's getting on my nerves."

"Leave Mother alone, Dietrich," interrupted one of the women. "You're always on at her."

The old woman put the knitting down on her lap with shaky fingers. "I don't like the sound of what you're planning." Her voice was querulous. "It'll land you in prison, if not worse. I wish you'd not got mixed up with that Axel; he's a bad lot."

Dietrich glared at her. "Shut up! You want things to change, don't you? We have to find a way to make that happen."

She lapsed into silence, still shaking her head.

"Well, I think we've covered most of the essentials," he continued, making notes in a large folder in front of him, "but what we need to think about now is a fall guy, someone the Stasi can pick up instead of us while we cover our tracks."

His wife considered for a moment, gave a little laugh, then looked across at her sister. "I think you might know just the person, Jutta. Couldn't you get her over here? It might be in your interest, too."

Jutta's thin lips tightened and she was silent at what she saw as a provocation.

"Don't start that again you two. Let's stick to essentials." Dietrich lit another cigarette.

Jutta got up and pushed her chair back impatiently. "I'm tired, I've had enough of this for the moment and I'm going to have a drink and then get on with some work. Let's continue this later this evening." Before Dietrich or her sister could say anything more, she left the room, slamming the door behind her.

"Now look what you've done, Kristina," grumbled the old lady. "She'll be in a bad mood all evening now."

Dietrich shrugged his shoulders. "She should get a life, make more of herself and find somebody else instead of moping around all the time."

Kristina sighed. "No, that was stupid of me to keep picking at her like that. The trouble is that poor old Jutta's never got over Nicholas—still hankers after him."

Dietrich frowned impatiently, got up and strolled towards the kitchen. "I'm going to get myself a beer—want one, Kristina?"

She shook her head. "Perhaps later with supper." She went over to the window, drew back the frayed, worn curtains and stood there for a moment, deep in thought. The little street was deserted apart from a sad-looking dog nosing around the cobbles, searching vainly for food.

"I still think it's worth dropping more hints to Jutta when she's in a better mood. It could kill two birds with one stone. I've just got to remember to be more diplomatic. What do you think, Lotte?" She turned to look at her mother-in-law, but the old lady had nodded off to sleep over her knitting. The ball of wool had rolled across the rug. Kristina smiled affectionately and stooped to pick it up. She removed the knitting gently from the bent, gnarled fingers and placed it on a stool beside the rocking chair. Lotte stirred and murmured something in her sleep.

Poor old thing, she thought, *caught up in all of this. We just must try and make things better for all of us. Our plans have got to work.*

Dietrich put his head round the door. "I'm going out for a bit. I've got a meeting—I'll be back in about an hour."

Kristina sighed. "It's that Axel, I suppose. I agree with your mother. I really don't like that man. Does he have to be involved in all this? You let him dominate you too much."

"I know what I'm doing. You worry too much," her husband replied irritably. She heard him pick up some papers, and the front door slammed shut before she could say any more.

Chapter 3

Maggie Stewart swore softly as Richard's tractor rumbled and rattled noisily through the farmyard past her caravan, waking her from an uneasy sleep. She groaned and pulled the duvet over her head. Trust Rick to choose this particular morning to start up so early when she'd had such a bad night. The crisp October air blowing through the open fanlight penetrated even the thick duvet. With a sigh, she peered at her watch—7 a.m. She fumbled for her slippers and the heater switch, the welcome heat soon filling the small caravan as she gazed tired and depressed out of the window at the farmyard beyond. With another sigh, she turned towards the sink and filled the kettle.

"Stop feeling so sorry for yourself. Pull yourself together. You're being pathetic," she said aloud. "You'll feel better after you've got a cup of coffee inside you."

Her voice trembled, faint and unsure, despite the confident words. She suddenly felt very alone, in need of company, or at least the sound of another human being. She switched on the radio, but the familiar soothing tones of John Humphries only reminded her of home. She heaved another gusty sigh and peered at herself in the small mirror over the sink. The face that stared back at her looked drawn and weary, her fair hair tousled after much tossing and turning and her grey eyes puffy with dark shadows. She examined her face more closely and thought that she could see yet another couple of lines. She had aged ten years in the last few weeks, she thought. She sat down heavily on the bed, clasping the mug of coffee she had just made, and wondered what her options were now. What was even more dispiriting was that everything had all seemed so positive when she first arrived in Oxford.

"Why did I ever come here?" she moaned aloud. "I should've taken that gap year to Australia like Jenny told me to. I could be sunning myself on some tropical beach right now instead of having to face that wretched man every week with his caustic comments." She swirled the half-cold coffee round in the mug.

He makes me feel so small and inadequate, she thought miserably, *it's as if I'm a ten-year-old back at school, being told all the time that I could do better*.

Maggie Stewart knew that she had reached a crossroads in her life. She really needed this fresh challenge to be a success, and to start with, she hadn't had many problems. Living in Oxford as a student had all seemed so different from her former life—so stimulating, so exciting, so full of adventure. She'd felt she was coping well with this new existence. Even things she'd been worried about had turned out to be easy in the end.

"Your sense of direction is hopeless," her sister had teased her. "Heaven knows how you'll get on in Oxford!"

But one of the porters at college had soon reassured her.

"Oxford's a small town," he said kindly on her first day. "The centre's just a mile or so of crowded streets. Walk up St Aldgate's turn into Cornmarket, then stroll along Broad Street to Blackwell's or the Bodleian, then you're nearly back at college. Most places you'll want are either grouped round there or St Gile's." He smiled at her anxious face. "Look, here's a map to get you started. Just relax and enjoy yourself."

I will. I certainly will, thought Maggie.

Then, there was the caravan. She hadn't used it for years. Too many painful memories, but setting it up on her own had been surprisingly easy. She knew, the first time she set eyes on the mellow, old farmhouse and the orchard nearby with one or two caravans dotted around, that she had been very lucky indeed to discover this small site so close to the city. Appleton Farm was a peaceful spot. It lay deep in the Oxfordshire countryside, nestled in a valley and protected by the trees planted by Richard's great-grandfather. Maggie's caravan was parked right beside the farmhouse, and Richard's mother, who ran a Bed and Breakfast there, had been extremely kind when Maggie arrived, towing her little caravan and looking rather apprehensive. She had bustled around, helping her to settle in, and even brought out some tea and homemade cake. This all had made her feel very welcome.

"Now, don't forget to ask us if there's anything you want, Maggie," she said. "Rick's always around if you've got a problem with the caravan or your car."

Maggie was grateful for the homely atmosphere of the place, and though she had to fend for herself, this was certainly a much cheaper option than living in college. After a few false starts, she found it an easy drive to the nearest 'Park and Ride' car park at Seacourt, and the frequent bus service dropped her right in the centre of Oxford. At first, she had slept soundly and woken up, raring to go and looking forward to the new day and the challenges that lay ahead. The drive from the farm to the dual carriageway that lead to the car park was something she really enjoyed because as the road climbed steadily, she could see the spires of Oxford in the valley below. It was a thrill to think that this was where she was heading. Now, however, as she had grown more and more anxious, this pattern had been broken, her feelings of inadequacy replacing her former happy optimism.

"I wish I was back in London," she mused aloud, nursing the empty coffee mug. "I could be looking forward to lunch with Jenny or Sue and then a bit of retail therapy, and perhaps, even a trip to the theatre."

The reality of a crisp, sunny autumn morning should have raised her spirits, but all she could feel was a dragging sense of depression. She longed for that early light-heartedness that she had felt when she had first begun her studies in Oxford. Lack of sleep had left her feeling headachy and gritty-eyed. She'd spent most of the night tossing and turning, dreaming that she'd missed some vital lecture or other, and that Professor Stowkovsky was telephoning her to demand an explanation. The insistent ringtone from her mobile made her jump.

"Hi, Maggie, this is your early-morning wakeup call!"

Maggie laughed reluctantly. "Angie, this is early even for you—you've got me at a bad moment. I feel really rotten this morning." She visualised her friend, short and plump, probably sprawled on her bed in her college flat, overlooking the Mansfield Road. "Don't try to be polite. Dumpy is what I am, darling," Angie had said cheerily when they first met at one of the first MCR drinks parties.

"Is it that old professor of yours, again?"

"Oh, Angie. I had such a rotten time yesterday with him. I feel like giving up, I really do."

"You can't do that, Maggie. How will I get through my D.Phil. without you? Let's meet up for coffee later, and I'll hear all about it. I've got a seminar soon, so I'd better rush. See you elevenish in the JCR."

Although Angie's call had cheered her up a bit, the memory of yesterday's bruising tutorial with Professor Stowkovsky came flooding back and made her want to slide under the duvet again. She could recall every moment of that disastrous session and his first words as she sat down in front of him at the large oak desk piled with files and books.

"That's banal!"

"What is?" Maggie had asked in disbelief and with that all-too-familiar sinking feeling of despair that she always felt during these personal sessions.

"This statement here about the role of the narrator." He stabbed his finger on the offending passage already liberally besprinkled with red biro. She felt a knot of tension tighten in her stomach and wondered why she had come to Oxford at all.

Yet, when she had been offered the chance to do a Master's degree as a mature student, she had been overjoyed. Her interview had been tough, and when, at the end of an hour's grilling, the Dean had said she would recommend Maggie for a place, her initial feeling had been one of total disbelief followed by an overwhelming joy that someone really believed that she was capable of achieving the high level demanded. She hadn't been happy with her life for some time—two failed relationships and being made redundant at the relatively early age of fifty had not helped her self-esteem, and she had felt the need for a fresh challenge in her life.

"You're getting in a rut, Maggie," her sister Jenny informed her brutally soon after her retirement. "You've got a good pension now. You can please yourself with what you do, so why don't you take up something totally different? Have a gap year, go trekking round South America or fruit picking in Australia."

Maggie looked at her sister as she stood by the bedroom mirror, taking the curlers out of her long brown hair, her clothes strewn over her bed in the usual disorderly way.

"You're a bossy boots, Jenny, do you know that? And why don't you tidy up a bit?" she observed.

"Takes one to know one," her sister retorted, "and you're changing the subject."

Maggie laughed reluctantly, but she had to admit that her sister had a point. She was independent now and could do whatever she wanted. She mulled it over for a few weeks, thinking about various options. When she was still working, she'd never had much time to focus on some of the things that really interested her. Her first degree was in Russian and German, and the target of doing a Master's would be a very stimulating goal, even more so if she could get into Oxford. She'd been hankering after this for years but never had the time or money. Now she had both.

When she put the idea to her sister, Jenny was very enthusiastic.

"That would be right up your street, Maggie. Go for it! A couple of years at a university like that would certainly put a stop to your drifting into this middle-aged rut."

Maggie bristled at her younger sister's frankness but recognised the truth of what she was saying. She did need to shake up her life.

A couple of years at Oxford will certainly do that, she thought. The M.Phil. sounded daunting in the prospectus, but she really wanted to succeed and had arrived at Oxford in late September for the Michaelmas Term, apprehensive but determined to give it her best. Now, her best did not seem anywhere good enough.

Her first fraught meeting with her supervisor was now over three weeks ago, and yesterday's piece of work was the third assignment she had produced for Professor Stowkovsky. She had laboured for hours in the college library with books piled up on her table, and she'd felt quite pleased with the result. This time, unlike the previous two assignments, she was sure he would be full of praise. On the contrary, he had seemed unable to find anything good to say. She stared at him dispiritedly across his large oak desk.

"Have you actually studied your Tolstoy?" he demanded, pushing her work back to her across his desk. She had put in hours of study on the required works and all the source material she had been able to track down in the Taylorian. It appeared useless to inform him of this, so she simply stated, "Of course."

"Well it doesn't seem like it. Take this away," he continued, pointing at the offending work. "Have a look at some of my suggestions and see if you can come up with something rather more original and not simply a rehash of the source material you've read. By next week, please."

He nodded his dismissal. As she closed his door behind her, the student waiting his turn asked nervously, "How is he today?"

"Not good," she muttered.

"Never is these days."

She made her escape down the narrow, winding stairs and out into the late autumn sunshine. As she walked down Turl Street, she began to wonder if she should admit defeat and abandon her Oxford dream.

Nicholas Stowkovsky curtly dismissed his last students of the day, and as the door closed behind them, he turned to the window and stared unseeingly out at the night sky. He had pushed that dreadful letter to the back of his desk drawer, but not out of his mind. He did not need to get it out, though it was more than three weeks now since it had arrived. He knew the words by heart and had agonised over them ever since. Not for the first time in his life, he was tortured by doubt and indecision. He didn't know what to think, what to believe. He ran his fingers impatiently through his dark hair now liberally streaked with grey. He felt he had failed his wife as he had failed his mother all those years ago.

"I should have made more time for Heike. I shouldn't have let her go off on that foolhardy trip," he told himself for the hundredth time. He had been responsible for her. He knew the dangers she might face. 1989 had not been a good time to go to East Germany with all the unrest earlier in the year, but she had been so determined. The harsh words he had spoken before she left now returned to torment him. He frowned as he thought back to that time at the airport. Although it was more than two years ago now, the scene was as fresh as if it were yesterday.

His wife's sad, wistful face haunted him. He had known that she wanted to heal the rift between them and wished he would say the loving, forgiving words that he found impossible to utter after their bitter quarrel of the night before. He had simply planted a brief kiss on her cheek and, ignoring her beseeching look, had turned away without a word, leaving her alone in the long, snaking departure queue. How he regretted that now. How could he have been so unforgiving, so unloving towards someone he loved so much?

He thought again about that cruel, unsigned letter. Was it conceivable that Heike had harboured Stasi sympathies? A myriad of questions raced through his mind. Could she have been recruited before they met? Had she been a spy here in Oxford, sending information back to East Germany? She had been patriotic, certainly. They'd had many arguments about the nature of that regime and some of them had been bitter. But a spy...could he have been so totally unaware? Impossible, surely. A worse thought struck him. Might she have married him simply to gain access to his colleagues and friends?

Perhaps, Heike had been deceiving him all along and had only pretended to love him to secure a recruiting base here in England. He felt an intense stab of pain at the thought. No, he couldn't bear even to contemplate that possibility. He just longed desperately to have her here in his arms, reassuring him with her love. Now, if the unknown writer had been telling the truth, he wondered if he would ever see her again. It was this 'not knowing for sure' that was so hard to bear— so many months without any news until the arrival of that wretched letter. He had stuffed it in a drawer because he could not bear to read it again, though every malign word was burnt into his memory. He now did not know what to believe. It was as if the wife he had known had never existed.

He rested his forehead against the cool windowpane. "Heike," he whispered despairingly, "why did you have to go?"

Chapter 4

The watchers were still in their place the next day. The black Trabant with its two occupants was parked as usual just across the street from her apartment. Heike Stowkovsky forced herself to continue her normal early-morning tasks before sitting at her desk to continue work on her thesis. It was no good. She was compelled to get up and check yet again that they were there. She knew that every time she peered out, they would note her pale face and anxious blue eyes at the window and register a certain victory. They were wearing her down with this constant surveillance. The first day or two, she had been able to pretend she did not care. She had even gone out to the car with some coffee and sandwiches. She had tapped on the car window, and when it was wound down, she saw that the two men were younger than she had expected—early twenties, perhaps. They could almost have been her sons if she and Nicholas had ever got round to having children—too late now, of course, though with her high cheekbones and elfin features, she looked younger than her fifty-three years. They shook their heads as she offered the refreshments she had brought and made no response when she had said lightly, "I'll be going to the university in a few minutes and will be there all day—no point in waiting here."

She walked back across the street, trying to appear nonchalant until she reached the privacy of her apartment, when she realised that she was trembling uncontrollably. She forced herself to drink the coffee and eat the sandwiches that she had made for her tormenters. As she left the apartment block with her briefcase, she tried not to look across the street to see if they were watching her or, worse still, following her. How many days was it now? Could it have been connected with that recent visit to Lotte's house? Impossible, surely—it had been such a harmless request. Her thoughts flicked back to that evening. She had felt guilty that it had taken her so long to fulfil her promise. She had been in Jena a fortnight already, but there had been so much to do settling in. She now decided that she had to deliver the package entrusted to her. When she had left the university with Jutta's letter and a slim parcel safely tucked in her bag, the early evening sunshine was so pleasant that she had decided to walk rather than take a tram. She stopped briefly to check that she had Jutta's directions.

"You don't mind delivering this for me, do you, Heike?" Jutta had asked the day before Heike left for Jena. "It's Lotte's birthday soon, and she was such a wonderful supervisor and helped me through some difficult moments."

"No, no, of course not," Heike had assured her, "It'll do me good to have a break; can't study all the time. I'd like to meet Lotte, anyway."

She had not thought it necessary to mention the affair to Nicholas—he didn't seem to care for Jutta much and avoided her whenever possible—"An old disagreement" was all he would say when pressed. Neither had she told him how many times she and Jutta had met up for coffee or lunch when he was busy. She did feel a bit guilty sometimes about keeping it secret, but she and Nicholas usually ended up arguing if they got on to the subject of East Germany. It was one link she and Jutta had, and why shouldn't she chat occasionally about her own country and in her own language? It gave her less of a conscience when she thought that. After all, she and Nicholas often spoke Russian at home. No, she decided, it was easier to keep quiet; what he didn't know couldn't hurt him.

As she made her way to the older part of the town, the streets became narrower and the street names harder to distinguish. She was not helped by the fact that the daylight appeared to be fading. As she looked up, she could see that dark clouds were filling the sky, and there was an ominous rumble of thunder. There was hardly anyone around to ask, and when she spotted a woman approaching on the other side of the road, she crossed over to ask where Torgasse was. The woman averted her eyes and hurried past, simply shaking her head.

It was late August, and there was a sense of nervous expectancy in the air, Heike reflected. The recent demonstrations in Leipzig, though peaceful, had created a feeling of tension. There were so many rumours, with news trickling the back of floods of East Germans fleeing across the now porous borders into Hungary. There were even whispers that the East German administration was discussing the possibility of relaxing the restrictions on their citizens when they wanted to cross through the checkpoints at the Wall.

Suddenly, she spotted Torgasse—a tiny, cobbled street, more an alleyway, on each side of which were small, narrow-fronted houses with wooden shutters. As she turned down it, heavy drops of rain started to fall. She peered through the gathering gloom and realised that she had reached her goal. Having checked the envelope to make sure it was number 18, she knocked on the heavy oak door, and the sound seemed to echo around the narrow street. There was no response, and she knocked again—louder this time. She looked up at the tall, narrow façade, identical to the others around it—there were heavy net curtains at the small windows, and she thought she saw one twitch slightly as if someone was observing her. As she stepped back to get a better view, the movement stopped, and she then wondered if she had imagined it. The rain was falling steadily now, and she was getting soaked in her thin coat. It seemed pointless to knock again—after all, she'd only wanted to say hello to Lotte. Before slipping the package and letter through the letterbox, she stood for a moment, undecided, feeling the parcel and wondering what might be in it.

I suppose I could put a message on the back of the envelope, she thought. She rummaged in her bag for a pen and scribbled a few words. She quickly added her name and telephone number. The rain was making it difficult to write, and her fingers were slipping on the pen, making her writing a bit uneven, but it was clear enough. She hurriedly pushed letter and package into the letterbox. "If Lotte wants to contact me now, she can," she said to the empty street as if there were listeners behind every door.

Her mission accomplished, she hurried back the way she had come. Actually, she was quite glad to leave Torgasse. It had taken on a sinister feel in the gathering gloom, and she still had a feeling she was being watched. She only relaxed when she reached the town centre again. She was wet through by this time and cold as well, so it was with relief that she turned down Goethestrasse where her apartment was situated. The block of flats was grey and featureless, as were so many in East Germany, and her apartment felt cold and unwelcoming with only the bare essentials for day-to-day living—but it was quiet, cheap and convenient for the university. As she opened her front door, the telephone was ringing.

She half-hoped it was Nicholas, but it was unlikely—the connection was bad outside East Germany and was often cut. *No, it's probably Marta*, she thought, *checking up I've not forgotten about tonight.*

Marta, tall, dark and elegant, was one of the few friends she'd made since she'd arrived in Jena and, much to Heike's relief, had approached her early on. Heike, who was finding the suspicious atmosphere hard to overcome, was grateful for her support. She found Marta a bit reluctant, though, to talk much about herself. She was vague about her past, apart from admitting she'd been teaching at the university for some time. What puzzled Heike a little was that she seemed to know quite a lot about her already.

"Did you ever meet Jutta Volk?" Heike asked her once, thinking that was the connection. "She used to study here." But Marta, after a short pause, had simply shaken her head.

They had arranged to meet up for a drink later, and Heike was expecting to hear her clipped, precise tones. However, when she answered the phone, the caller, after a slight pause, put down the receiver. Heike stood undecided for a moment, wondering if it would ring again, but when it did not, she went to change out of her wet clothes. She felt vaguely uneasy but tried to shake off her feelings of disquiet.

"Probably a wrong number," she told herself as she washed and changed—the water was cold again, but that was all a part of the austerity suffered under the East German regime.

"I'm imagining things. It's so easy to be suspicious the way things are here."

Like everyone else, she was well aware that the Stasi, the state security, had set up a web of undercover agents—colleagues informed on colleagues, friends and family on those close to them. It was often done through fear, a subtle pressure of threats, or through the conviction that this Communist state was truly a bulwark of resistance against Nazism and Western corruption and greed. Heike had found herself being observed warily when she arrived.

Although she was East German by birth, her parents had escaped to West Germany in the late fifties, and from there on to England. Her father, a bookseller by trade, and her mother a teacher, had decided to settle in Oxford, and it was there that she had met Nicholas. She now had a British passport, making it possible for her to travel more or less at will across the border between East and West Germany, and this, she was sure, generated envy and perhaps even hostility at the university in Jena. However, one or two members of staff like Marta had been a little more welcoming.

"I'm only going to be here a couple of months," she told herself firmly. If she really focussed on her research, she reckoned she could put up with the situation for that short time. She tried to push out of her mind the sneaking suspicion that perhaps Nicholas had been right after all. She was never going to let him know that, though.

Later, as she and Marta chatted over their drinks at a bar just around the corner from the university, she mentioned her walk to Torgasse and how wet she had got.

"Hard to believe now." She sipped her wine appreciatively as she glanced out of the mullioned window. Its panes, coloured and decorated in dark amber and red, reflected the skill of Jena's glass-working traditions.

The storm earlier had given way to a pleasant, starlight night, promising fine weather for the following day. She thought Marta looked at her sharply as she mentioned Torgasse and the reason for her visit. When she heard Lotte's name, her eyes narrowed, though she asked no more questions. Heike felt a restraint in her manner, however, and she refused Heike's offer to buy her supper.

"Sorry, Heike, no time tonight. I've got a seminar to prepare for and student essays to mark for tomorrow."

She hurried away with a brief wave, and as Heike sat over her solitary meal, she could not throw off the feeling of unease that she had felt since leaving Lotte's house earlier that evening.

I wonder what was in the package, she thought, *I wish now that I'd simply put it in the post.* She pushed her food around on her plate. Suddenly, she seemed to have lost her appetite. Cradling her wine glass in both hands, she stared thoughtfully at the red wine as it swirled to and fro. It was strange, perhaps, that Jutta had been quite so pressing in asking her to try and make contact, and then to let her know how Lotte was keeping. She had told Heike so many stories about her studies and how wonderful Lotte had been to her that Heike's curiosity had been aroused.

"She'll be a useful person for you to meet," she assured Heike. "She might even be able to help you in the research you want to do."

Two days after her visit to Lotte's house, the Trabant had arrived in Goethestrasse.

Chapter 5

The first formal dinner in college had seemed to Maggie like an improbable dream. She walked with the other students, dressed for the first time in her Oxford graduate gown, white shirt, with a little black ribbon tied at the collar and a dark skirt. *Any moment*, she thought, *someone's going to tap me on the shoulder and say, sorry, there's been a mistake and you shouldn't be here at all.* She looked up at the Oxford spires silhouetted against a moonlit sky, the windows of the college library glimmering in the moonlight, and stopped for a moment just to take it all in. Suddenly, she heard a giggle behind her, and someone grabbed her arm.

"I can't believe I'm really here, can you?"

Maggie turned round with a start and laughed when she saw who it was. "You made me jump, Angie!"

"Don't we look impressive, darling?" She twirled around and nearly knocked over another student just behind them. They both collapsed in helpless giggles as he glared at them before marching off down the cobbled path.

"He's terribly starchy, that one," observed Angie. "Never smiles, takes himself really seriously."

"Certainly can't accuse you of that," said Maggie, looking at her friend affectionately.

She and Angie had formed an immediate bond. Both in their fifties, they shared many of the same interests. Angie had a lively, laidback personality. She was always ready with a joke or a bit of gossip, which lifted Maggie's spirits when she was starting to find her studies hard-going. She was always teasing Maggie about getting too worked up about her difficulties. "For goodness' sake, relax and enjoy yourself while you can, Maggie. Just think, we could stay on here as perpetual students if we play our cards right. You haven't got any ties now. Why don't you find yourself a nice boy toy?"

"You must have a very tolerant husband, Angie," Maggie observed one day when she had got to know her better. "Leaving him behind in Reading with three children. How on Earth does he cope?"

Angie had shrugged her shoulders carelessly. "He complains sometimes, but I don't take any notice. They'll manage, I expect; after all, the children aren't babies anymore."

That was typical of her easy-going, happy-go-lucky personality, Maggie reflected. After a few weeks, they built up a routine that on formal dinner evenings, they would go into the Ashdown together. It was a magnificent dining hall dating from the sixteenth century with a high, arched ceiling, the oak beams blackened with age. Above the ancient, stone fireplace hung a portrait of the previous principal of the college, and the soft glow of the fine, stained-glass windows contrasted with the old oak panelling. John, the High Steward, who was in charge of catering, was a dark, rotund, jolly little man and enjoyed joking with them.

"I'm going to christen you 'Absolutely Fabulous'," he had informed them after a couple of weeks, "You can work out who's Joanna Lumley."

Maggie and Angie looked at each other and chuckled.

Angie, who only just came up to Maggie's shoulder, ran her fingers through her blonde, spiky hair streaked with platinum and sighed theatrically. "No prizes for guessing who's Joanna, then," she said.

John smiled and topped up their glasses. He liked them both, and it hadn't taken him long to realise that they not only really enjoyed the marvellous wines on offer but were also quite knowledgeable behind all the banter, so he always kept them well supplied.

A college renowned for its well-stocked cellar is a plus, thought Maggie appreciatively after that first evening.

On the Wednesday evening following her bruising encounter with Professor Stowkovsky, they sat in the Ashdown as usual, waiting for the principal and his guests. Maggie confided in Angie that she almost felt like giving up. "Nothing I do ever seems right," she complained.

She reckoned she'd been very unlucky in the appointment of replacement supervisor. Alexandra Lewinsky, who was the original choice, had been suddenly taken ill. *She'd sounded so charming over the phone*, Maggie thought wistfully. Professor Nicholas Stowkovsky was not at all charming; quite the reverse. Maggie discovered later that he'd planned a sabbatical for that year and was presumably resentful at having to be responsible for this mature student who seemed to be incapable of producing work of the required standard. Her very first meeting with him had not been a success, either. She had been nervous as she climbed the narrow, winding stairs to his study. His gown and a jumble of books and papers on the small chair outside his door seemed to indicate he was there, but when she knocked timidly, there was no reply.

After a moment's hesitation, she opened the door and saw a tall, dark-haired man having an acrimonious conversation in Russian with someone on the telephone. He was standing near a window which looked out over the dome of the Sheldonian to the Bodleian library beyond. A distant church bell chimed four o'clock. As she was absorbing all this, he became aware of her presence and swung round. His dark eyes glared at her as he waved an imperious hand to signal she should wait outside. He kept her waiting for about ten minutes before he flung open the door and pointed to a chair on one side of his large oak desk. As he sat down opposite her, he said coldly, "Kindly wait in future until I open the door."

She had muttered an apology as he rustled some papers that seemed to contain notes about her.

"I see you did a part-time degree in Russian," he said, consulting the papers on his desk, "and only obtained a 2.2." Then abruptly switching to Russian, he continued, "So what grasp do you have of the spoken language?"

Maggie, already unnerved, was so taken aback at this sudden change that for a moment, she could only stare at him, before muttering, "Good enough, I think."

She had, in fact, spent six months in Russia on an exchange and had a good grasp of the language, but at that moment, all her vocabulary seemed to fly out of the window.

"Well, I hope it's better than good enough," he replied crisply, switching just as abruptly back to English. "You'll have to read many books in the original language."

He then proceeded to give Maggie her first assignment and a very long book list and dismissed her by saying, "Right, this time next week please."

"Are all supervisors like this?" she asked a fellow student the next day in the JCR after telling him about the terrible time she'd had.

"Some are," he told her with all the wisdom of a first year behind him. "What gets them really scratchy is if something crops up and they suddenly find they've lost that sabbatical they'd been planning. I sometimes think we get a bit short-changed here, anyway. There's not really a lot of contact time—something to do with being self-sufficient, independent learners." He gave a hollow laugh as he headed back to the library. Maggie gazed after him, feeling rather depressed.

She sighed gustily as she remembered all this and reminded Angie what she'd had to put up with.

"He certainly sounds like a real pig," Angie observed, "but you mustn't let him get to you. Let me have a good look at him sometime, and perhaps, we'll make a wax model of him and stick pins in him—that will polish him off!"

Maggie giggled—Angie always managed to make her laugh however low she felt. At that moment, the principal entered and they all stood. Maggie suddenly noticed that Nicholas Stowkovsky was among the guests processing up to the top table. He looked sad rather than glowering, she thought, as he sat next to the principal.

"I must say, he's considerably handsomer than the old bean I've got," whispered Angie incorrigibly as Maggie pointed him out to her.

"Can't say I've noticed," grimaced Maggie. "He's always glaring at me."

Three or four glasses of wine later, though, Maggie's spirits were uplifted enough to grin at Professor Stowkovsky as he walked out after dinner. Maggie thought that he looked startled, and a muscle twitched in his cheek that might have passed for a brief smile.

"There you are," said Angie. "Probably a real pussycat underneath that grim exterior."

The next morning, Maggie sat ensconced in the college library, surrounded by reference material. 'Nesting', as it was called, was forbidden, but all the students quick enough to establish themselves sat at their chosen table tucked into the cosy alcoves lined with the well-thumbed books in the beautiful old library and soon made themselves at home. Some left a sweater or two draped over their chair. Even a duvet and books were left propped open as if their owner had just popped downstairs for a coffee. Maggie chewed thoughtfully at her pen. She really wanted to produce something different this time. Something that would make even Professor Stowkovsky say was a good or even a passable piece of work, anything rather than the scathing dismissal of her previous efforts. This had to be more innovative. She looked again at the assignment he had given her at her last tutorial: 'How far might the work of Tolstoy be seen to represent the issues of his day?'

"This, I hope, is wide enough to prevent you from merely lifting ideas from your secondary sources," he had said in that dismissive manner that Maggie had come to dread.

She thought about the German studies she had done with the Open University three years ago. One author who had really gripped her imagination had been Christa Wolf, an East German writer who had produced many works during the forty-year period when East and West Germany were separated with the foundation of the DDR, the German Democratic Republic, in 1949. Christa Wolf believed in the Socialist system but not the way in which Ulbricht and then Honecker, with Russian support, were controlling their people behind the Wall, which they had erected in 1961. In her novels, there were coded criticisms of the administration and its state-controlled security system—the Stasi.

Maggie considered carefully. Perhaps, she could do some kind of evaluative study and comparison between Tolstoy and Wolf and the two systems of government. She thought for a moment and decided to go downstairs to the JCR, grab a cup of coffee and see if she could find someone to chat to about her ideas.

"I know," she thought as she made her way downstairs. "Sebastian—he'd be just the person."

Although he was a good bit younger than Maggie, they had formed a bond built up on all their mutual interests, particularly languages and social history. As Sebastian came from Leipzig, he could fill in a lot of gaps for her about the history of East Germany. They frequently spent evenings together in the college bar, chatting and arguing, him polishing up his already impeccable English and Maggie struggling to improve her rusty German. Initially, he had appeared shy and reserved and difficult to get to know, but little by little, he relaxed in Maggie's company and proved to have a wicked sense of humour. Maggie enjoyed ribbing him, particularly about the European Community which she hated and wanted Britain to pull out of, whereas he, with eyes on a job in Brussels, fervently supported the whole concept.

"What a waste of money," she'd say mischievously.

"How can you say that!" He'd start to become indignant until he saw she was teasing him yet again.

She was in luck. He was sitting there in his usual corner, a cup of coffee beside him, half-hidden behind the morning paper, his thin, dark face adorned with his customary tiny, black-rimmed glasses. They gave him a serious air and made him look older than his years, Maggie thought.

"Just the person I wanted to see," she called out to him. Startled, he appeared from behind his paper, then smiled when he saw who it was.

"Maggie, hello! Come and join me. What can I do for you?"

After pouring out a cup of coffee, Maggie sat beside him.

"Sebastian, you've read a lot of Christa Wolf, haven't you? What do you think of this for an idea?"

She explained her ideas and why it was so important to get it right this time. He knew all about the problems she had been having and sympathised with her, only too relieved that he had a much more easy-going supervisor. He was very encouraging and supportive, and after an in-depth chat, Maggie returned to the library with renewed enthusiasm. This time, she would definitely show Professor Stowkovsky that she could produce a piece of work up to his exacting standards. After several trips to the Bodleian and the Taylorian libraries, she went back to her 'nest' again and started work in earnest. She refused all of Angie's blandishments to come and have a coffee and a gossip and worked through the rest of that day and well into the night in the caravan. When she was satisfied that it really was the best she could produce, she walked down Turl Street the next day and slipped her assignment into Nicholas Stowkovsky's pigeonhole. She had to now try to relax and enjoy the weekend ahead. Saturday was to be a red-letter day—matriculation for all new students was the day you became officially a member of Oxford University.

It was a beautiful, crisp October morning as the students in their formal attire, their gowns billowing out behind them in the slight breeze, emerged from the various colleges and processed through the streets of Oxford to the Sheldonian where all the major ceremonies at the university took place. Maggie gazed up at its beautiful dome as she waited in the sunshine with Angie and Sebastian. The pavement outside Blackwell's bookshop was lined with TV cameras, the local press and scores of interested sightseers. Once the students were all safely seated inside, the Chancellor's procession—a riot of scarlet and gold—would make its stately way through the Oxford streets and into the Sheldonian.

Later that night, Maggie lay on her bunk with a myriad of images flashing through her mind—the serried rows of her fellow students, the dome of the Sheldonian rising above their heads, the sense of history and the sonorous voice of the Chancellor. "You are among the privileged few fortunate enough to attend this ancient institution, but privilege brings responsibilities." After the ceremony, the students trooped back to their respective colleges for a buffet lunch and group photographs on the lawns. A truly wonderful day Maggie, thought as she drifted off into a deep sleep in which she dreamt that her supervisor was congratulating her on her brilliant piece of work.

As Nicholas Stowkovsky started looking through Maggie's assignment, he realised with a sense of shock that she had alighted on the very topic that had interested his wife. "Why Christa Wolf?" he muttered to himself as he reached out for Maggie's file and glanced through her record details.

He should, of course, have realised from that file where her interests lay, and he felt that he was not focussing on his students as he should, preoccupied as he was with his own concerns. He recalled Maggie's happy, glowing face as she sat above him at the matriculation ceremony, her light-hearted joshing with her friends at dinner the other night. It had made him feel twice her age, but he realised from looking at her notes that she was only a year younger than him. He envied her obvious enjoyment of her Oxford life, though he probably was not adding to it with his sarcastic reception of her work. He knew that he had lost his zest for life over the past couple of years since Heike's disappearance. Taking off his glasses, he got up from his desk and went over to the window. He picked up his wife's photograph from the bookcase and studied it carefully. With her short auburn curls and blue eyes, she was vivacious rather than beautiful, and it was this vivacity that had attracted him over thirty years ago, though he wondered now how well he had really known her.

He realised with a sense of shock that he was already putting her into the past tense. That wretched letter had certainly done its work. Lord knows he had tried to find her. Perhaps he had been wasting his time, and she had been dead all along. All those trips he had made to Jena, all those meetings with an uncaring East German bureaucracy and the university personnel—they had all been to no avail. It was as if Heike had vanished off the face of the earth. There was mention of 'undesirable connections' outside the campus, though no one was prepared to say what or who they were. A visit to Heike's apartment had revealed nothing— it lay bare and empty. His wife's possessions were available for collection at the university, he had been informed, and the apartment had just been re-let.

"Without rent being paid, we can't afford to leave the apartment empty. There's too much pressure for accommodation here," he was told curtly.

With the opening up of the borders with the west a month later and the unification of Germany the following year in March 1990, Nicholas had hoped that the search for his wife might become easier, or even, hoping against hope, that she might just turn up in Oxford one day with a reasonable explanation for her disappearance and lack of communication. However, as the days went by, he began to lose that hope and had begun to come to terms with the fact that his wife had fallen foul of the authorities in those final turbulent months of East Germany's existence or she had seen this time as an opportunity to leave him and their life together in Oxford. Closing his eyes, he visualised all the possibilities.

"I can't just give up. I want to know for sure, but where to start?" he mused aloud.

He sighed and, replacing the photo, returned to his desk and picked up Maggie's work again. He read it with increasing interest—she had really enjoyed writing this, he thought, and although there were some areas he could criticise, nevertheless, it was original and well-researched. Having written some comments that he hoped were helpful, he gave the assignment 60%, put it into an envelope marked 'to be collected' and left it at the porter's lodge on his way home.

As Maggie got off the bus the following morning, she walked down Turl Street and, hoping against hope, went into the lodge and asked the porter if Professor Stowkovsky had left anything for her. She had lain awake most of the night, wondering if this time, she might make the grade and had decided that if her work got yet another scathing rejection after so much effort, she would probably throw in the towel. The porter examined the pigeonholes behind him and then smiling, handed her the familiar large brown envelope. Maggie hurried out into the street again and tore open the envelope with trembling hands. Hardly able to believe her eyes, she saw the magic 60%, and her heart leapt with joy. She was so overcome with relief and the feeling of achievement that she did not see someone coming towards her until they collided, and she looked up with a start as she stumbled against the tall figure of her supervisor. He steadied her with his hand on her arm, and looking down at her face glowing with happiness, he noticed her assignment clutched in her hands. His dark eyes twinkled as he smiled at her.

"You are obviously pleased with your result, Maggie," he observed quizzically.

"It was such a relief after so many failures," Maggie stammered, suddenly shy, not only with his rare use of her name but also the sudden contact.

"What made you decide to explore East German literature?" he enquired, curious to hear her reply.

Emboldened by the encouraging tone of his voice, Maggie answered without hesitation, "I really found it fascinating, studying the authors' observations about people's lives in these two German states, separated for so long, one of which was a Russian satellite. Each in its own way had time to develop characteristic features and Christa Wolf..."

She wondered if she should continue. Nicholas gazed down at her for a moment, her eyes alive with enthusiasm. With a sudden pang, he recalled Heike's face similarly glowing the night before she left for Jena.

"It's something I really want to do, Nicholas," she had said. "The whole concept of that society and what their writers are trying to achieve really fascinates me."

It was useless trying to dissuade her as she brushed aside his feelings of unease.

"Anyway, you'll have Jutta to take care of you in the couple of months I shall be away," Heike had said teasingly. "I think she's always had a soft spot for you!"

Nicholas shuddered at the thought—he found Jutta's manner creepy in ways he could not explain even to himself, though he had liked her well enough at one time. Her pale blue eyes reminded him of a cold fish, and he felt she had influenced Heike in her decision to go to East Germany.

Maggie had stopped speaking mid-sentence. There didn't seem much point in continuing; Professor Stowkovsky appeared to be in another world.

Suddenly, he turned away from her. "Make sure you keep your focus on the Russian literature your M.Phil. is aimed at," he said abruptly. And with that, he turned into his college entrance and vanished from her sight. Maggie gazed after him, his sudden change of mood bewildering and surprising her.

Two evenings later, she confided all this at dinner with Angie while John topped up their glasses, joking with them as always.

"I really don't understand him at all, Angie. One minute, so charming and interested, the next so abrupt."

"Well," said Angie after a sip of wine, "I've heard some gossip about your supervisor. Apparently, his wife Heike went off to East Germany a couple of years ago to do some research and never came back."

"You mean she simply vanished?" exclaimed Maggie incredulously.

"No one knows exactly," continued Angie. "She was either abducted or murdered or simply decided it was a good opportunity to abandon her life here—after all, she was East German, you know."

"Perhaps, she found herself another man," said Maggie. "Poor Nicholas."

"Oh-ho—Nicholas now, is it?" laughed Angie as John topped up their glasses again.

Maggie blushed and refused to be drawn further, but she mulled over this information as she walked back to the bus later that evening. She had a tutorial with her supervisor tomorrow afternoon and wondered if there was any way of finding out more. But she could hardly blurt out, "Oh by the way, do you know what's happened to your wife?"

She wondered how he would be after their unexpected meeting in Turl Street, but his manner was brisk as he discussed her assignment and dismissed her with a curt nod after giving her the title of the new one. This allowed no reference to Christa Wolf or East Germany, Maggie thought, as she made her way wearily along Broad Street and down past St Giles on her way to the Taylorian Slavonic library to get the necessary secondary material. Her nose wrinkled as she considered the new title: 'The changing role of the narrator in the work of Tolstoy'. It was as if Nicholas Stowkovsky did not want her delving into that area of research that she had touched on in her last piece of work. Perhaps, it was somehow connected with his wife or simply brought back painful memories. Nevertheless, Maggie's curiosity was aroused, and she was determined somehow to try and unravel the mystery of Heike Stowkovsky's disappearance.

Chapter 6

Nicholas poured himself a large whisky and sat down in his favourite chair by the fire. He stared thoughtfully into the flames. *It's been a hellish day*, he thought to himself. He'd reduced one student to tears at his final seminar of the day and the meeting with the Dean had seemed endless. "Never knows when to stop, that woman," he decided as he took another sip. The first thing he'd done when he got in was to get the fire going. He needed the comfort and warmth of it particularly tonight. Paula had left him one of his favourite meals, a steak and kidney pie with all the instructions, clear enough even for him, but at the moment, he just couldn't be bothered. Sue next door had found Paula for him when she realised Heike wasn't coming back.

"A real treasure you'll find her, Nicholas. She helped us out when I broke my leg last year and just couldn't cope. She'll do everything—whatever you want. Otherwise, you'll end up living in a pigsty and eating at the pub every night."

Certainly, he knew he couldn't have managed without her—she cleaned, did the washing and prepared tasty meals. All he had to do was switch on the oven or shove something in the microwave. He finished the whisky and closed his eyes. Any moment now, he would drop off to sleep, but there was something he really couldn't put off any longer. "She met a fitting end for a Stasi sympathiser," these words had been festering in his mind for over three weeks. He dragged himself out of the chair.

He hated himself for what he was about to do. "What if, what if?" Always that corrosive question running through his mind. "What if Heike had been..." he could hardly bear to put it into words, "... an informer? Perhaps, she'd been persuaded somehow or even forcibly pushed into a role of reporting back useful information." Jutta's name flashed into his mind; she and Heike had certainly seemed pretty close. Or perhaps, Heike had fallen for another man. He felt a wrenching pain at the thought of her making love to someone else.

"She was attractive enough, damn it," he said aloud as he wrenched open one drawer after another in Heike's desk in a corner under the stairs—what she'd laughingly called her 'Arbeitsecke'—her little work corner. He'd touched none of her things since she'd left, like a talisman, that she'd soon be back. He felt like a spy himself as he leafed through her papers. They were mainly notes from lectures she'd been to, typed copies of assignments for her degree work, letters from her parents and valentines he had sent her. He felt grubby and ashamed, rifling through her personal things, but he had to know. There was nothing. He heaved a sigh of relief, though he knew the worst was to come. As he opened the door of their bedroom, he stood for a moment and looked at the bed where they had so often made love. He closed his eyes briefly, as if trying to blot out the memories before opening the doors of her wardrobe. A faint aroma of Madame Rochas lingered still on Heike's clothes. He searched each pocket and amongst her carefully folded sweaters—still nothing.

Why had he doubted her? He would surely have found something by now. There was only one other possible place. Most of her underwear had gone with her, he realised, as he opened the few small drawers of her dressing table. They were virtually empty, and he was just relaxing again. There was only one more thing to look at. He picked up the small, soft handkerchief sachet, embroidered by her mother when Heike was a child and one of her most treasured possessions. It was tied with a pink satin bow, and when Nicholas opened it, there he found it—what he'd been dreading. Hidden inside were two wafer-thin sheets of paper. His hands trembled. It was a typed list of names, some of which he knew but others totally unfamiliar. After each name were asterisks—one, two or three, some coloured. He could make neither head nor tail of it. He sat down heavily on the bed, feeling literally sick. There was probably some perfectly simple explanation, but he couldn't be sure; he couldn't ask her. How long he sat there, he didn't know. He lost count of time.

He looked at the list of names again. Could he ask some of those he knew whether Heike had asked them any particular questions? But how could he give a reason for his interest?"

After a while, he got up. He'd better put the papers back where he'd found them. Paula was in tomorrow, and he certainly didn't want her finding them. He walked down the narrow winding staircase like an old man, feeling a mixture of anger and despair. There was no one he could confide in—not even his sister, Alex, close as they were, or Sue and John, his closest friends. He just felt totally

"Thank you, Jutta, very thoughtful. By the way, have you met Marianne le Guen? She arrived at the beginning of this term as our Junior Dean and is doing some very interesting research on the Breton language and customs."

Jutta looked at Marianne with disfavour and barely acknowledged her murmured greeting.

"What are you doing after our drinks party, Nicholas?" she asked. "Would you like to come back to my place for supper?"

Nicholas tried to suppress his rising irritation. Would the woman never get the message that he was just not interested?

"Thank you, but no," he said firmly. "I already have plans."

He refused to be drawn on what these were, for fear that she might invite herself. Sue and John, his neighbours in Cumnor, had suggested going along to a recital of Christmas music being held at the Holywell Music Room later that evening. Nicholas, who loved music and was himself a very competent pianist, had gladly agreed. To avoid further questioning, he moved away as soon as he decently could, saying he had to speak to the principal. He felt a pang of conscience leaving Marianne to Jutta's tender mercies, but he wasn't in the mood for crossing swords with her this evening.

Jutta, despite a sense of annoyance at the rebuff, tried not to reveal her feelings too openly. She was only too aware that some of her colleagues would have been eyeing the exchange, and she did not want either their pity or their amusement. Fortunately, Marianne also made her excuses a few minutes later, saying she was having dinner with her boyfriend, who was over in England for the weekend. Jutta breathed a sigh of relief. At least that saved her from having to pump Marianne to see if her evening plans involved Nicholas.

She did not speak to him again that evening, but on her way back to St Giles, where she rented a house with Julia Streeten, one of her faculty colleagues, she reflected bitterly on the halcyon days as a student when she and Nicholas seemed so close. Before that wretched woman, Heike, came on the scene, she thought, slamming the front door behind her and throwing her keys with a clatter on the hall table. They'd shared so many evenings at the Oxford Playhouse or one or other of the numerous cultural events that were on offer in Oxford. Often, Nicholas would come back to her room for a late coffee and a chat about what they'd just been to. He always kissed her on both cheeks as he got up to leave, and Jutta longed for him to put his arms around her and kiss her with more than the friendly but rather distant affection he always showed.

"Go for it, Jutta," Julia, her college friend, had advised her when Jutta confided her frustration. "You've been going out together for about three months now—it's certainly about time he made a move. Perhaps he doesn't know how you feel—so show him."

The twenty-year-old Jutta considered her friend's advice as she lay in bed that night. She was relatively shy and inexperienced as far as men were concerned, and this was the first time she had really been in love. This was definitely not what her tutor at Jena had intended when she advised her to spend this year at Oxford to perfect her English, she thought ruefully. She'd not intended to get involved romantically, but the moment she met Nicholas and looked up at his lean, dark face, she felt her heart lurch and she was lost. As a seasoned Oxford graduate now working on his D.Phil., he seemed much older than his twenty-four years, his dark eyes often serious and reflective behind the steel-rimmed glasses he sometimes wore. Like her, he was also based at Mansfield College and had stopped to help her one day when he saw her in the library, struggling with the intricacies of the inter-library access on the computer. He then took her under his wing, taking pity on her confusion with all the very individual peculiarities of Oxford life.

"Oxford can make you feel very inadequate indeed," he told her kindly. "Just focus on what it is you want to achieve and make the most of all the riches on offer here."

However, it was not long before Jutta decided that what she really wanted was to make Nicholas fall in love with her, though that seemed easier said than done. He was warm and friendly but made no real physical contact. He never invited her back to the barge which he shared with another impoverished student.

"Far too spartan," he informed her early on in their acquaintance. "Do you know there was ice on the duvet when I woke up this morning!" He chuckled ruefully at the memory.

I wouldn't mind being under that duvet with you, ice or no ice, Jutta had thought wistfully, but hadn't dared say so. Now, three months later, she was becoming impatient and was determined to take Julia's advice. That evening, as she and Nicholas walked back to her room at college, she asked him up as usual for a nightcap.

"You're really lucky being able to afford to stay in college, Jutta," he said as they went into her spacious study bedroom in one of the older wings of the college. "The East Germans must be very generous with their funding."

"I suppose we are lucky," agreed Jutta as she made hot chocolate for them both. "If you are gifted in any way—in sport for instance—it's relatively easy to get finance. I'm so glad I live in East Germany—we are really spoilt as academics with funding, a guaranteed job and accommodation." She paused, her pale cheeks glowing with enthusiasm.

"But restricted freedom," observed Nicholas wryly, looking rather amused.

"Well, I'm here, aren't I?" said Jutta as she carried two steaming mugs over to the coffee table. But she did not want to get into a political argument tonight. She knew the views that Nicholas held about her country well enough. She sat down beside him as close as she dared, but he made no effort to touch her. Instead, he began talking about the lecture they had just been to together. When he rose to take his leave, he lent forward to kiss her on both cheeks as usual. Without stopping to think, Jutta turned her face, and with a beating heart, placed her lips on his. For one glorious moment, she thought he was going to return her kiss, but instead, he pulled away from her.

"I'm very fond of you, Jutta, but not in that way. I'm sorry," he said with his face averted.

With that, he pulled on his coat and left without saying any more. Jutta was left in the middle of the room, shaking with both desire and anger. Things were never quite the same between them after that evening, and Jutta regretted her action. She tried to raise the matter one day when she caught him alone in the JCR, but he refused to be drawn on the subject and became even more remote. Soon, Jutta's time at Oxford came to an end, and she was forced to return to Jena to complete her degree. She had said goodbye to Nicholas, looking in vain into his dark eyes to see if there was any sign of a change of heart. She could not get him out of her mind, however, and as soon as she had successfully completed her degree, she applied for and got funding to return to Oxford to continue her studies.

On her arrival, Julia met her and took her back to her own temporary accommodation. She was now doing research herself, and although she was really pleased to see Jutta again, she was dreading this moment as she gently informed her that Nicholas was now married. Ashen-faced, Jutta collapsed on the nearest chair and questioned her further.

"Funnily enough, it's another East German," Julia informed her, avoiding her gaze and anxious to get this conversation over as quickly as possible. "She's been living in Britain with her parents, and I think they've all been given British

41

passports because it's too dangerous for them to return to the GDR—I've heard her father's some dissident writer in exile and that he's also a bookseller by profession, so he's set up his own bookshop in Broad Street. I gather Nicholas met Heike working there when he went in to buy something. It was all very quick—love at first sight, so they say."

Jutta felt an overwhelming, all-consuming hatred of this unknown woman who had taken her Nicholas away from her. She leapt to her feet and strode round the room, beating one fist into the other.

"I could kill her," she burst out with a violence that made even the phlegmatic Julia look really worried.

"Now, steady on, Jutta," she said kindly but firmly. "He really wasn't yours for the taking, you know. He as good as told you so. You've just got to accept it."

"Never," retorted Jutta, her pale eyes blazing with anger. "What can she give him that I can't?"

Julia wisely refrained from answering her but went to the fridge and took out a bottle of champagne.

"Look what I've got to celebrate your return to Oxford," she said as she put the bottle and two glasses on the coffee table. "Let's make plans—I've found a nice little house to rent in St Giles if you'd like to share it with me. I've been lucky enough to get funding, and I'm sure you have, so we should be able to afford it. What do you think?" And she pushed the estate agent's details across the coffee table towards Jutta. "Come on now, old thing—why don't you sit down and look at this while I open the bottle? There are plenty more fish in the sea, you know."

Jutta, though still shaking, did as she was bid, and after a couple of glasses of Veuve Clicquot, managed to get some semblance of control, much to Julia's relief. She was able finally to agree with her friend about the St Gile's house, and they moved in the following week.

Jutta was now dreading the first meeting with Nicholas, and it came sooner than she had expected. Hurrying down Broad Street on her way to Blackwell's bookshop, she spotted them—the familiar figure of Nicholas with his arm round the shoulders of a small, auburn-haired woman. With a sick feeling in the pit of her stomach, Jutta saw Nicholas bend and kiss his wife on the lips.

Chapter 8

It was about 7.30 when Nicholas Stowkovsky left Jesus College and hurried down Turl Street towards Broad Street. He was heading for the Hollywell Music Room situated not far from the King's Arms—a favourite student haunt—and on this particular night, filled to overflowing with students celebrating the end of the Michaelmas term. He'd arranged to meet John and Sue just outside the chamber concert venue. He glanced at his watch; he'd cut it a bit fine.

The temperature had dropped several degrees, and it wasn't an evening to be hanging about outside. John Winterton, the local doctor, and his wife, Sue, had been good friends of both his and Heike's for many years, and the four of them had shared many happy occasions together. John and Sue still included him in all their plans, and for this, Nicholas was eternally grateful. Although he had many friends at Oxford, it was good to get away from academia, sometimes. He also felt freer and more relaxed with them when talking about Heike and his doubts and fears about the possible reason for her disappearance. Just offloading some of his worries at that time had helped him through some of the unbearably dark days when all contact with her seemed to have been lost.

Close friends though they were, however, two things he couldn't bear to reveal to them were the contents of the anonymous letter and that list in Heike's dressing table drawer. Anyway, as he still hadn't decided what he should do, he pushed the memory of these firmly to the back of his mind. This evening was certainly not a time to be dwelling on such painful subjects. He'd drunk rather more than usual at the party, and this had gone some way towards dulling unpleasant thoughts and fears. But seeing Jutta at the party tonight had reminded him of the influence she had seemed to exert over his wife.

"Could she have been the recruiting agent?" he wondered as he crossed over Broad Street. Heike's closeness to Jutta definitely wasn't all his own imagination. He remembered past conversations with John and Sue; they'd obviously noted it too; it wasn't just him.

"I certainly think Jutta seemed to exercise quite an influence over her, Nicholas," John had observed during one of these early discussions. "She's a very strong, dominating sort of woman, isn't she? Heike often spoke about her in a way which made me feel that Jutta was someone she really… how shall I put it?" He paused and considered carefully. "Someone she looked up to."

"I'm convinced that Jutta was behind Heike's decision to continue her research in Jena," Nicholas had said bitterly. "I tried to point out to her that the wealth of research material here in Oxford was second to none, but she was absolutely fixed in her determination to go. Jutta studied at Jena herself, you know, and filled her head with all the stories about how wonderful it was studying there." He broke off, remembering all the arguments he and Heike had had on the subject, and his face clouded over with the memory of it. Sue, seeing his unhappiness, had tactfully changed the conversation to something more general.

When Nicholas had gone home later that evening, John raised the subject again. "What I don't understand is why Jutta made so much effort in drawing close to Heike. You'd have thought she'd have disliked her intensely for taking Nicholas from under her nose."

"But Nicholas was never hers for the taking," disagreed Sue. "For him, she was always just a friend."

"Jutta had other ideas, though. She's one very determined lady. I've always felt she'd stop at nothing to hook him. I don't think Nicholas ever realised quite how smitten she was. Perhaps, she was responsible for Heike being spirited away."

Sue, though fiercely loyal to Nicholas, could never agree with John on this. She'd always felt rather sorry for Jutta, whom she saw as an introvert, a withdrawn personality who was always on the fringes, finding it difficult to make contact with those around her apart from a select few. *Perhaps, Germans are always on the defensive*, she thought to herself, *as if they're still under suspicion even after all these years.*

From then on, John and Sue had made a real effort to try and help Nicholas come to terms with the unexplained disappearance of his wife and to organise events they knew would give him pleasure, like this pre-Christmas recital at one of their favourite venues. Holywell Music Room was a quaint, low, white building, chapel-like in appearance. It was shabby but charming, and its intimate setting attracted a faithful following, situated as it was in Holywell Road right in the centre of Oxford and near to so many colleges. Nicholas spotted his friends waiting for him and quickened his stride.

"No hurry, Nicholas, you're in plenty of time," called out Sue as he drew nearer. A small, dark woman with short, curly hair, she barely reached Nicholas's shoulders as she reached up to kiss him warmly on both cheeks.

"A typical Oxford party, eh?" observed John, smiling as he shook him by the hand, "I scent a good rich claret there."

Nicholas laughed. "One glass seems to lead to another at these pre-Christmas events—you should've come. I did invite you."

"Someone has to drive us back to Cumnor," smiled John as they made their way inside. He was a tall, gangly figure with twinkling blue eyes and a shock of red hair still only just tinged with grey. A quieter individual than his wife, with a gentle, roguish sense of humour, he seemed content to live in the shadow of her bubbling, extrovert personality. In reality, he was the one she turned to constantly for reassurance and advice.

"My, it's full tonight," observed Sue as they sat down. "All the usual here as well as a few new faces."

The programme on offer was an interesting mix of Baroque and early twentieth-century music, many pieces with a Christmas theme. The trio, all in their early thirties, took it in turn to introduce each item, giving a little background history, often with a humorous anecdote about the composer.

"The violinist is brilliant," said Sue as they had coffee and a sandwich in the interval.

"She's from Poland," said her husband, looking at the programme, "and she's been making a living up till now working the cruise ships with the other two."

"Rather a waste," suggested Nicholas, biting into a smoked salmon sandwich. "I certainly wish I could play as well as that pianist; his Chopin solo was breathtaking."

"Don't do yourself down," said Sue firmly. "You're an excellent pianist."

"Not up to that standard," laughed Nicholas. "Do either of you want more coffee or sandwiches?"

"No, thanks. I think we ought to start going back to our seats," said John. "Anyway, Sue's got a nice little supper lined up for when we get back."

The trio finished their recital with a special arrangement of 'Silent Night' and Nicholas closed his eyes as he listened, remembering that this was Heike's favourite carol.

As they all emerged into Holywell Road, snow was falling gently, dusting the ancient rooftops and glistening against the floodlit facades. A distant bell chimed 10 o'clock.

"So beautiful," murmured Sue as they made their way to the bus stop in the High Street, "and very appropriate after that lovely music."

"Though not very silent," joked her husband, pointing at a lively group of students emerging from Exeter College, clutching gowns and bottles of wine and heading noisily down the road to a neighbouring college. "There are obviously going to be some parties tonight."

The three of them waited outside Ede and Ravenscroft for the Seacourt 'Park and Ride' bus. The snow was falling more heavily by this time, the wind blowing it into small drifts against the ancient facades.

"Only every half hour at this time of night," shivered Sue, pushing her hands deep into the pockets of her coat. "Hope we haven't just missed one." But just at that moment, the number 400 came lumbering into view.

"What are you doing for Christmas, Nicholas?" asked John as the bus rattled past the railway station. "Are you going up to your sister's in Scotland as usual?"

"Yes," replied Nicholas, "I'll probably take my skis in case there's some good snow. Alex and Bill have a lodge up in the Highlands as you know, so we might get some skiing over the New Year."

It was snowing even harder as they got off the bus at the terminus, and the cars were already covered with about an inch of snow. As they neared John's Volvo, Nicholas noticed a woman standing beside a car with the bonnet up. She looked vaguely familiar, and he suddenly recognised Maggie peering desperately into the engine.

"Is there anything we can do for you, Maggie?"

The familiar voice made Maggie jump. She looked up and saw his concerned face, dark hair dusted with snow.

"My car just won't start, and I think I've now run down the battery," she said, her voice unsteady with the anxiety of being stranded in a dark car park late at night. Nicholas, seeing her face tired and strained, felt a sudden rush of compassion. Without thinking, he grasped her arm firmly and led her over to where John and Sue were standing by their car, looking perplexed.

"You get into the car with Sue," he said reassuringly after introducing them to her, "and John and I will see if we can get your car started."

Maggie protested feebly, but still overcome by his sudden appearance and his unexpected sympathy, she meekly did as she was told. John cast a sideways glance at Nicholas, wondering who this Maggie might be, but his friend offered no explanation as they tried in vain to get Maggie's Fiat going.

"The leads are damp from the snow blowing into the radiator, I reckon," suggested John. "We'd better tow her car to our place and then see if we can get it started with jump-leads."

Maggie was too relieved and grateful for their offer of help to put up any resistance. Before long, they arrived safely in Cumnor, and Sue ushered her unexpected visitor into their little thatched cottage.

"I think we should all have some supper in front of the fire before trying to get the car started," she said firmly, raking the stove and getting a cheerful blaze going. She brushed aside Maggie's protests about not wanting to be a trouble. "John, darling, I'm sure we could all do with a large whisky. Maggie's hands are frozen." And with that, she bustled out to the kitchen and soon re-emerged with a trolley laden with soup and large platefuls of quiche and sausages. John meanwhile dispensed the whisky which Maggie gratefully accepted, feeling at last some warmth in her cold fingers as she stretched out in front of the fire. The whisky started taking effect, and she began to relax in the unexpected situation she had now found herself in. She wondered what Angie would say if she could see her now sitting in this lovely old cottage in the company of her feared prof and his friends who were all proving to be so kind and welcoming, doing their best to make her feel at ease.

"Where are you heading for, Maggie?" asked Nicholas curiously as they all sat round together in front of the fire, enjoying Sue's ample supper.

"Back to Eaton where my caravan is parked on a farm campsite. I decided it was a cheaper option living there rather than in college," she added defensively, seeing their surprised faces.

"Well... this is a coincidence. You must be staying at Rick Salter's place," interjected John. "He's the only farmer who has caravans round here. Do you remember going up there for a shoot last year, Nicholas, and we brought back a brace of pheasants for Christmas?"

Maggie grimaced as she recalled the pheasants hanging up in the shed near her caravan, their beautiful, glossy feathers gradually becoming dull as the days passed.

"You obviously don't like pheasants," observed Sue, seeing the look on her face.

"I'm afraid I'm a bit of a hypocrite," admitted Maggie. "I love to eat them, but I don't like to see them killed and then hanging in front of me with their beauty gradually fading away every time I go to the shower."

"I'm the same," agreed Sue. "I'd definitely rather see them ready for the pot—I certainly couldn't pluck them. John has to do it before I'll even go near them."

They all laughed, and Maggie felt as if she'd known them for a long time. Even Professor Stowkovsky didn't seem quite so formidable as usual. She wasn't really sure how to address him—the others of course were using his Christian name, but she somehow didn't feel able to do that. Yet, his title would have seemed too formal under the circumstances. *I'll play safe and avoid using either*, she thought.

Nicholas remembered his barge all those years ago, and his eyes twinkled. "It must get pretty cold in a caravan in the winter. Do you ever get frost on the duvet?"

Seeing Maggie's bewildered face, John laughed and told her the story of Nicholas in his student days living on the river. Maggie, though she was having difficulty in imagining her supervisor as a young, light-hearted student, also laughed. "Not yet, though the caravan door stuck this morning with frozen condensation, and I had to take a run at it. And the Calor gas had frozen, so I couldn't even make a hot drink!"

"You poor thing!" exclaimed Sue. "Well, if it happens again, you just pop down here and I'll make you a large, cooked breakfast."

The mention of breakfast and the caravan made Maggie glance at her watch, and she saw to her horror that it was by now well after midnight. She realised that she really shouldn't trespass on their hospitality any longer.

"I wonder if I ought to get a taxi rather than bothering you with my car tonight," she ventured hesitantly.

"Nonsense," said Nicholas firmly. "We'll soon get your car going. I'll go next door and get the jump-leads from my garage, and then we'll follow you to the farm to make sure you get back safely."

"I couldn't possibly put you to that trouble," protested Maggie, but John and Nicholas had already left the room.

"I wouldn't try arguing with Nicholas," laughed Sue. "He's a very determined man when he's made up his mind to do something."

"I'm just beginning to realise that," murmured Maggie, still absorbing the fact that she had unknowingly been passing his house each day on her way to the bus.

"How did you get to know him?" inquired Sue, who had been longing to ask all evening.

Maggie explained that she was one of his students and for some reason felt a telltale blush at the rather quizzical look in Sue's eyes. Fortunately, she was saved from any more questions by the return of John and Nicholas bearing the good news that her car was now running and that it had stopped snowing. After thanking Sue, who kissed her warmly and told her she must come again, she set off in the Fiat up the lonely country lane to the farm with the two men following in John's car. They left her outside the caravan and, brushing aside her profuse thanks, disappeared down the farm track on their way back to Cumnor.

Maggie, now safe and warm in her caravan with her precious car tucked away in one of the barns, went straight to bed. As she pulled the duvet over her, she smiled as she reflected on the surprising turn of events that evening and Nicholas Stowkovsky's unexpected concern. *He seemed almost human*, she thought to herself as she fell into a deep, dreamless sleep.

Chapter 9

Heike had decided to put Lotte out of her mind; a fortnight had now gone by since her visit to the house in Torgasse, and she'd heard nothing. Anyway, she had too many things preoccupying her at the moment without thinking about Jutta's old supervisor. What was bothering her was the progress of her research—it really wasn't going as well as she would've liked. The main problem was that she was constantly preoccupied about being under surveillance. It was on her mind the whole time, and she just couldn't focus.

The black Trabant was back in its usual place this morning, and although she was making real efforts to ignore it, she still felt a cold lurch in her stomach as she peered out first thing in the morning and saw it there. This morning, though, was a good morning—it was crisp and bright and the post brought a letter from Nicholas. He was not a good letter-writer, and the envelope had obviously been opened by the censor, but this was commonplace in East Germany at this time, so she wasn't too worried about that. It was just comforting to see his familiar scrawl and get news from home, even though there was a certain restraint in his manner.

She felt the ache of homesickness as she read about his plans for the new academic year and how he'd had their sitting room redecorated. She shut her eyes and visualised the little village of Cumnor, their old stone cottage and Sue next door, calling over the hedge to see if she would like to come in for coffee. She felt her eyes pricking with tears which she brushed away impatiently. She had chosen to do this, after all, and she was determined to see it through. Sitting at the kitchen table, she cradled her coffee cup in her hands and gazed unseeingly across the bare little room. She and Nicholas had had so many arguments over her proposed trip. Despite her UK passport, he argued in his usual forceful way that it was a dangerous time to go to Jena and that she should do her research in Oxford. It was a crazy idea to put herself in unnecessary danger when East Germany was in such a volatile state. She was forced to admit (though only to herself) that he had good reason to be concerned.

In June 1988, Mikhail Gorbachev, the Soviet leader, had declared that there should be more freedom of choice for the countries in the eastern bloc. So, there would be no more Soviet military force as support for governments like those in the German Democratic Republic. Up till then, there had not been very much overt opposition because of the Stasi, but by 1989, all this had changed. By mid-1989, Leipzig's Nikolaikirche had become a focus for peaceful demonstrations as people protested against travel restrictions.

"You're a fool to go at this particular time," Nicholas had said to her.

"But I've got a British passport. I'll be fine." Heike felt her temper rising at his domineering manner.

"With all the demonstrations taking place, you may find that even a UK passport is no help," Nicholas retorted.

"If Gorbachev hadn't interfered and decided to initiate glasnost and perestroika, there wouldn't have been any problems," countered Heike, though she knew she was being irrational as she was only too aware of the unacceptable restrictions being placed on East German nationals.

"If the Russians hadn't been supporting all these Communist regimes, they would have collapsed years ago," replied Nicholas ironically as he picked up his briefcase and left for a meeting.

They had argued again a few days later when Nicholas questioned why she couldn't do her research in Oxford.

"When I've finished my research, I particularly want to go on and visit Christa Wolf's hometown, which is where I was brought up," Heike said wearily. "I've told you all this before. I feel a special affinity with her, which is why she's the subject of my research. She and her parents went through the same terrifying ordeal that I did with my parents as they fled the approaching Russian army. We were so afraid, those Russians were worse than wild animals as they raped and murdered and showed no mercy to defenceless German civilians." She paused and put her hand to her mouth as she realised with horror that she had crossed a forbidden, unspoken boundary, and what a sore subject this was for the two of them.

Nicholas's face froze, and his dark eyes were cold as he snapped, "You Germans deserved all you got particularly when you think of the way my people were treated."

He went out, slamming the door behind him and did not return until later that evening. When Heike had attempted to heal the rift, he said icily that he did not want to discuss the subject again, and if she chose to put herself in danger, that was her decision. This frostiness lasted right up to the time she left for Germany with no physical contact between them, though their longing for each other sexually had always been so strong. He drove her to the airport, and Heike ached for him to put his arms round her, tell her he loved her and would be thinking of her. But he simply carried her bags to the check-in, kissed her briefly on the cheek and walked away without a backward glance.

Heike realised that her tears were now dripping on his letter. She wiped her eyes with her handkerchief and got up to tip her cold coffee down the sink. As she put the kettle on to make a fresh cup, she thought she heard a noise at the front door. When she went to investigate, she saw that a square, white envelope had been pushed under the door. Putting on the safety-chain, she opened the door and peered cautiously through the narrow gap. There was no one there, so she unfastened the chain, opened the door wide and stared down the dim corridor— no one, not a soul. She refastened the door and ripped open the envelope. Inside was a single sheet of paper. The writing was unsteady as if written by an elderly person. She glanced at the signature—the letter was from Lotte, asking her to tea the following day.

Heike sat at the table again, thoughtfully sipping her fresh coffee—the invitation seemed innocuous enough and referred to Heike as a friend of her dear Jutta. Heike had to admit she was curious, and Jutta had spoken of Lotte in glowing terms, urging Heike to make contact with her if she could. Her spirits sank again as she remembered that this had been yet another bone of contention with Nicholas. He had disliked her friendship with Jutta, and when she'd said she wanted to bring her home for supper one night, he'd shaken his head and told her in no uncertain terms that he did not want that woman in their house. He refused to be drawn further on the subject but had brought her an enormous bouquet of red roses that evening as if to make up for his brusqueness.

He was such a dear, thought Heike wistfully, and she recalled the first time they met in her father's bookshop. She had asked if she could help him, and when he looked down at her and smiled, she felt as if the whole bookshop had turned upside down. The flash in his dark eyes told her that he, too, had felt that instant, overwhelming attraction, and when he had invited her out, she had accepted without further ado. Within two weeks, he had proposed to her, and when she protested half-heartedly that they hardly knew each other, he grasped both her hands in his and told her that they had the rest of their lives for that.

When she broke the news to her parents, they were not very enthusiastic. Her father tapped his finger on the table as he always did when he was worried about something.

"This is very sudden, my Heike. You've hardly known him any time. Don't you think you should wait a little until you're sure?"

"But Papi, I couldn't be surer. The moment I saw him, I knew he was the one," protested Heike. She saw his face pucker with concern for her and felt a rush of love and worry about him—he looked so thin and wrinkled these days. The struggle with the East German authorities had taken its toll, she knew. He hated not being able to write as he wished without fear of censorship.

"And now, I'm a refugee again," he would say bitterly, "forced to leave my own land and live in a country that we were fighting not so long ago. They're still suspicious of us, I know." He looked at her again. "Think carefully about this, my little Heike." He paused and looked at his wife for help.

"Do you think marrying a Russian is such a good idea?" her mother said gently. "We like Nicholas, but there's been so much bitterness between our two countries—why not get to know each other better? Nicholas is only just finishing his D.Phil.—he needs to get a job first before he should think of getting married."

"Mutti, I want to be with him more than anything," Heike protested. "And I'm really sure about this. Our nationalities don't matter. We really love each other, and that is all that's important. The war is long gone; we've got to look to the future and try and forget all the terrible events of the past. We can't go on blaming each other in a new generation."

She knew her mother's thoughts were harking back to that harrowing journey they had all experienced as the war came to its violent close. That constant fear of the Russian approach was an abiding memory, and even though she had only been a little girl at the time, she recalled sensing her mother's terror as they packed as many possessions as they could into the cart, in which, in happier times, her father used to take the children for a ride, their little brown horse trotting along the country lanes with Heike as a toddler safely tucked between her father and her elder brother, Freddie. He had been forced to go to Berlin as part of the Hitler Youth Resistance force, helping to defend the city against the advancing forces.

"As if they stand a chance," Heike's father said bitterly. "It's just a waste of young lives trying to save that madman."

"Hush, my love," her mother said with alarm. "Someone will hear you."

"They're all too busy trying to save their own skins without worrying about us," he replied as he harnessed the little horse to the cart.

But Heike remembered the SS troopers who had come to their little town of Landsberg, rounding up all the young boys—many like Freddie, barely sixteen, and forcing them into army trucks.

"It's their duty to defend the Fatherland," all the distressed parents were told. "Anyone who resists will be shot." And they meant business, of that Heike was sure.

As they set off heading west, Heike and her parents had to travel a road thronged with others with all their worldly goods in bundles or carts. By nightfall, as they sheltered in a barn, they could see the sky lit up by flames from burning towns and villages to the east. Their only aim was to push on to where the Americans were in control. This had seemed ironic even to Heike as she had been told so often that the Americans were the enemy. The day they were told that the Führer was dead was when they started seeing Wehrmacht units abandoning their guns, secret papers and orders from HQ, and noticed strange, emaciated, ragged-looking people standing around by the side of the road.

"Mutti, who are these funny-looking men?" Heike remembered asking. Her mother had hushed her in a frightened whisper, and pulling her by the hand, had hurried her past. Heike later discovered that these wretched people were in fact former inmates just released from a concentration camp nearby and that they would've had every reason to have killed them without mercy with the weapons abandoned by the fleeing German forces. It was almost a relief when they were finally rounded up by the American forces before being resettled in Mecklenburg. It had almost seemed like a liberation.

Heike sat in her little kitchen in Jena, musing over all these memories and feeling once more the familiar stab of pain that she would never see Freddie again. He had been lost like so many others in that bitter, useless fighting on the streets of Berlin. Looking at Nicholas's letter as it lay on the table, she recalled their early days of married life. Their honeymoon had been a revelation to Heike. Nicholas, so tender and so loving, had swept her up into the heights of passion and joy that before meeting him she would have found unimaginable. As they lay in bed together on the first morning after their marriage, he had caressed her face tenderly.

"My dearest little girl," he whispered, "what happiness you've brought me." As he kissed her again, he pulled her into an embrace so passionate and so all-consuming that Heike felt her senses swim and the whole room fade away.

"I'm going to spend the rest of my life making you happy," he had promised her. "With me taking care of you, you'll never be afraid again. Once I'm a professor, we'll travel the world together." Heike had laughed, but Nicholas's face was serious as he reiterated that one day he would be an Oxford professor.

He had certainly kept his word as far as that was concerned, though they had not exactly travelled the world. He had grafted away and painfully made progress through the Oxford system until the coveted Chair was awarded to him. Heike sometimes felt that because of this burning ideal to make his way up the academic ladder, they had grown apart, and it was because of this that she had begun to study for a degree herself. Nicholas was proud and pleased when she attained a 2.1 in German literature and even more so when she was accepted to do an M.Phil. Was it now worth it? Heike shook herself out of her reminiscences and looked at Nicholas's letter again. It was affectionate enough, and he certainly said he was missing her—perhaps he was sorry that they'd parted so coldly, though he would be too proud ever to say so.

She looked at her other letter. *There's no reason why I shouldn't go*, she thought, *it'll stop me moping here worrying about things, give me something else to think about.* She was lonely, too; there was not a vast amount of companionship at the university, and Lotte had sounded warm and friendly, something that Heike really longed for at that moment. Perhaps, she could even confide in Lotte about the watchers. Heike shuddered; the term seemed to give a sinister significance to what was probably a normal occurrence for new residents at the moment. She picked up the letter again. Lotte had said not to reply if she was coming, and she made up her mind to accept.

Chapter 10

Maggie thought that the Hilary term was going to be a piece of cake after all her struggles in the autumn. She'd really enjoyed the last week of Michaelmas. All her assignments were in, and she could now draw a breath and relax. It'd been a fantastic time filled with parties and shopping for Christmas presents, but the high point had been the Christmas festivities at college when everyone's problems were forgotten as they joyfully sang carols together. Maggie's eyes were misty with emotion as she sat beside Angie in the lovely old college chapel. The principal's sermon was followed by the college choir singing all the traditional carols, and the whole congregation joined in lustily before trooping in to dinner.

The Ashdown Hall had been decorated for the occasion, an enormous fire had been lit in the lovely old fireplace, and there was a large Christmas tree beside High Table, its lights twinkling. The scent of the pine needles mingled with the rich aroma of the traditional meal being served. They all pulled crackers and behaved like a bunch of giggling, irresponsible teenagers rather than staid, mature students. John bustled round, dispensing wine and food and organising the grand processing of the traditional flaming Christmas pudding to loud applause. Angie and Maggie giggled as they watched Sebastian trying his first mince pie.

"I thought it was going to be full of meat," he protested, as they laughed at the expression of surprise on his face.

He even forgot his customary, rather formal shyness, and swooped on Maggie with a piece of mistletoe taken from the decorations and kissed her to loud applause from everyone round the table. Maggie subsided into her chair and sipped another glass of wine to hide her confusion.

After she had recovered her composure, she looked round the Hall and all the familiar faces, savouring the occasion. She felt a warmth of the togetherness and the shared tribulations that were part of student life. At that moment, she wouldn't have changed places with anyone in that glow of warm happiness.

Afterwards, she and Angie, wineglasses in their hands, impervious to the frosty night air, wandered round one of the dimly lit quadrangles in the snow, the ribbons of their gowns swirling around them as the east wind found its way even into that normally sheltered garden beside the old library. A full moon appeared briefly from behind a large bank of cloud that threatened further snow as Maggie recounted her adventures of the night before. Angie was wide-eyed as she listened.

"You mean you actually sat round the fire with him and swapped jokes," she gasped incredulously.

"Well, not jokes exactly," said Maggie defensively, "but he was very jolly, and of course, very kind in helping me like that. I don't know what I'd have done otherwise."

"Anyway, it's nice to know he's actually human. You'll probably find he'll be quite different with you next term," said Angie optimistically. "And you've got a lovely skiing holiday to look forward to as well, haven't you?"

"Yes, my brother Peter and his wife run a holiday chalet in the French Alps, and I usually help out over Christmas and get in some skiing as well," Maggie said.

"But I'll have to do a bit of study as well," she told herself as she drove back to London the next day. She'd received a daunting reading list through her internal mail that morning, and there was a large pile of books in the car that she'd thrown onto the back seat. One or two of them, at least, would have to be stuffed into her suitcase tomorrow.

The high spirits of early December had evaporated by the time Maggie came up to Oxford in the second week of January. Tanned and glowing after her stay in the high Alps, she was initially in an optimistic mood. However, she soon discovered that she was sadly mistaken in her belief that this term was going to be an easy ride. To begin with, a large proportion of her time would be spent on philosophy. "I know damn all about this," she realised with dismay as she looked at the term's programme. "I don't think even Sebastian will be able to help me out." The books on the reading list had turned out to be complex and abstruse, and she'd also discovered to her horror that she had to give a seminar later in the term to the Professor of Philosophy and the other M.Phil. students who were also doing Russian literature. It was a daunting prospect. She'd hoped her supervisor would give her some guidance. However, at her first tutorial with him after her return to Oxford, he was crisp and to the point.

"Any questions you may have regarding your philosophy studies should be addressed to Professor Cooper."

All memory of cosy chats round a blazing fire was obviously far from his mind, and Maggie looked in vain for some hint of change in his manner. He seemed as cold and impersonal as ever. The only relaxation in this starchiness came when she admitted that she'd not done as much work as she should have done and muttered rather lamely that she had spent too much time on the ski slopes. He appeared not to register this excuse, though there was a flicker of amusement and interest in his dark eyes as he informed her that he wanted her next assignment in by the following week.

"You are focussing on Dostoevsky this term, as you know," he reminded her, "and I suggest you discuss how his work is affected by his involvement with Utopian Socialism."

For what seemed like the umpteenth time, Maggie wondered with a sinking heart whether she'd been overly ambitious in attempting this degree. Oxford was definitely not for the faint-hearted, she thought as she made her way disconsolately down Turl Street.

After Maggie had left, Nicholas gazed at the empty chair where she had just been sitting. Why had he been so brusque? He could've been more relaxed with her just as he'd been on that evening just before Christmas. He'd really enjoyed her company once she'd relaxed in his presence, he mused. She had made him laugh more than he had for some time as she recounted her firsthand experiences of coming up to Oxford as a mature student and her thinly veiled references to some of his colleagues. He smiled as he remembered her story of her frozen caravan door and the row of dead pheasants outside the shower. He'd felt somehow on the defensive this afternoon as if afraid to drop the barriers he'd built up since Heike's disappearance. Perhaps he felt uncomfortable because Sue had made it clear that she liked Maggie.

"She's really nice, Nicholas; you must bring her round for dinner one evening," she had enthused the next time she saw him. Seeing the startled look in his eyes and the sudden stiffening of his body, she added hastily, "Only if you feel you can, of course, seeing that she's a student of yours."

Afterwards, John had ticked her off. "Don't start matchmaking, Sue," he warned. "Give him time to make up his mind about what he wants to do."

"He never will if he withdraws into his shell all the time," she said in her defence. "I think Heike has gone for good, and he needs to start making a new life for himself."

Nicholas had realised what Sue had been up to, and it had made him shy and awkward and he'd sought refuge as he always did by being stiff and impersonal. What had made matters worse was that Maggie had obviously expected him to be more friendly. She had greeted him with the same direct and unaffected smile as she had when she had thanked him as they parted that evening in December. There was a look of surprise in her grey eyes that made him regret his brusque and unyielding manner, and he almost gave in to an impulse to call her back. "That would be ridiculous," he told himself sternly. "It's far better to pretend that evening never happened."

As Maggie made her way back to college, she met Sebastian coming out of the tuck shop on the corner of Mansfield Road.

"You don't look very happy. What's happened Maggie, another session with the prof?"

"I feel really brassed off—fed up—miserable," she explained, seeing his puzzled expression. "That man is so moody and unpredictable! You can't discuss anything with him."

"What you need is a large cup of coffee, and then we'll walk down to the river and you can tell me about it," said Sebastian sympathetically.

Maggie protested that she didn't have time to go walking. "I've got a new assignment on Dostoevsky, and tomorrow, there's another philosophy lecture that I've got to read up on."

In the end, Sebastian persuaded her, and she poured out all her woes as they stood in the sunshine, drinking their coffee, before setting off through the narrow streets to Christ's Meadow. It was a beautiful, crisp winter day, and Maggie felt her spirits lift as they both walked down the long avenue that led from Christ College to the river beyond. Sebastian was such an easy-going, undemanding person to be with, a good listener, and he somehow seemed to put everything into perspective. When they reached the river, they walked along the towpath towards the Oxford boathouses in a companionable silence. The crews were out preparing for the boat race in two months' time, and their coach was running along the bank, yelling advice and encouragement.

"Have you ever done any rowing, Sebastian?" asked Maggie while they watched the teams straining to further efforts as they responded to their cox's instructions.

'I gave it a try last term," replied Sebastian as they retraced their footsteps. "You've got to be on the river before breakfast, though—wouldn't suit you, Maggie," he added, smiling, knowing how she hated getting up early.

Maggie slipped her arm through his as they walked down High Street. "You're such a good friend," she said gratefully. "Thank you for listening to all my troubles."

"It's a pleasure, Maggie, anytime," he assured her. "Look, why don't we go to a concert one night? There are a lot of good things on at the moment. You can't work all the time, you know, and it'll do you good to have an evening off occasionally.

"I'd really like that," she said enthusiastically. "You're right; it'd be a pity to tie up at Oxford and spend all the time with my nose in a book."

"I think there's a chamber concert at the Sheldonian on Friday. Do you want to go and check it out now?" asked Sebastian.

"I'm sorry, but I really haven't the time now," Maggie grimaced. "I ought to go and get some books out for the lecture tomorrow."

"Understood. Well, I'll go on my own then, and leave a note for you in your pigeonhole," promised Sebastian as they said goodbye.

Nicholas spotted them across the road as he came out of Flaggs Old College Store. He stood for a moment in the doorway, watching them, and frowned a little as Sebastian gave Maggie an affectionate hug and a kiss on both cheeks before they parted to go their separate ways. It shouldn't matter to him, of course, what she got up to in her private life, but there was a stab of jealousy when he saw Maggie's light-hearted wave as she walked off down the road, swinging her bag in a carefree way.

I used to be like that, he thought, *and now I've turned into a remote, crusty old professor*. He was beginning to wonder whether all this striving after academic success had changed him irrevocably, and perhaps it was this that had driven Heike to go her own way. That wretched letter was still in her dressing table drawer, and that was yet another unresolved problem. These gloomy thoughts accompanied him all the way back to Jesus College, where he proceeded to give his students a hard time at their afternoon tutorial session.

Meanwhile, Maggie set off for the Taylorian, feeling a new spring in her step. She even hummed a little tune as she scanned along the shelves, looking for some of the books on her book list for the philosophy lecture the following day. They were going to focus on Heidegger. Maggie wrinkled her nose. It didn't sound a very exciting prospect. *I'd better get some reference material for the Dostoevsky as well*, she thought to herself as she made her way up to the German language section, *or shall I leave the Russian material till tomorrow?* She stopped for a moment, undecided.

To get to the Slavonic library meant a longish walk past St Giles, carrying her philosophy books, and then, if she couldn't find what she wanted, she'd still have to go to the Bodleian. The only problem was that you couldn't borrow any books there, and copying was expensive because you weren't allowed to open the book out and copy double pages, in case you ruined the spine. Perhaps, she'd give that a miss today. Maggie sighed as she crouched down and began her search—so many customs and regulations to get used to here.

While she was looking, she suddenly spotted a name that seemed familiar— Jutta Volk. Maggie frowned and straightened up with the book in her hand. She looked at the title: 'The Importance of a Divided Germany'. Whatever was it doing in the philosophy section? Someone must have slipped it in there by mistake. She puzzled for a moment over the author's name. Where had she heard it before? Then she remembered that Angie, in her usual gossipy way, had told her that Jutta was an old flame of Nicholas's. "Before his wife came along…" she explained. "And then your prof dropped her, but I've heard that she still hankers after him."

Maggie sat down at a table and leafed through the slim volume. It had been written early in 1989, and quite clearly, Jutta Volk was totally against unification. It read more like a political treatise and was full of thinly veiled resentment about what she saw as interference of foreign powers in East Germany. Maggie looked at the flyleaf. There was very little information about Jutta except to state that she had graduated in Politics from the university of Jena and that she had attained her Doctorate at Oxford where she now lectured. She had written two more books: 'Politics and the State' and 'The Rise of East German' and also a number of articles. Maggie frowned. *Jena again*, she thought, *that name keeps on cropping up. I'm sure that's where Sue said Heike had gone.* She thought back to that evening in Sue and John's house. There had only been one jarring note when Sue had asked Maggie where she'd done her summer school for her Open

University course. As soon as she mentioned Jena, Sue unthinkingly blurted out that that was where Heike had wanted to go.

"Not until that wretched Jutta Volk encouraged her," Nicholas had muttered, his face like thunder, and John had hastily changed the subject.

"Jutta Volk is obviously not one of his favourite people," mused Maggie. "But then, I don't know that I am." She sighed and replaced the book in the German section. After about an hour of browsing, she finally left the Taylorian, weighed down with an armful of books, and made her way back down Broad Street.

The following day, Maggie decided to leave college a bit earlier than usual and drop in on Sue on her way back to the farm. She had brought back a large box of Swiss chocolates from her skiing trip as a 'thank you' for all John and Sue's kindness before Christmas. Sue's face lit up when she saw her at the door.

"I am glad to see you, Maggie. I've been thinking about you and wondering how your skiing trip went. Come in and have a sherry and tell me how you're getting on."

"Are you sure I won't be in the way?" Maggie asked, though she'd been half hoping Sue would invite her in. She wanted to find out a little more about Jutta, something about the woman interested her.

"No, of course not. John won't be in until 7 p.m.; he's got evening surgery tonight," replied Sue, sitting Maggie firmly down in front of the fire. She brought in the sherry decanter and a couple of glasses, and when Maggie presented her with the chocolates, kissed her warmly on both cheeks. "That's really sweet of you, Maggie, but there was no need. We really enjoyed our evening with you. Now tell me, how has the new term been so far? Is Nicholas still giving you a hard time?"

Sue proved to be a good listener, and Maggie gave her an abridged account of all her difficulties, trying to be as tactful as possible about Professor Stowkovsky.

"That philosophy option can be a real bind," Sue agreed sympathetically. "I remember Nicholas telling me he had problems when he was doing his graduate studies."

"Then you'd think he'd be a bit more understanding," Maggie said without thinking and then bit her lip. "Sorry, I didn't mean…" She trailed off, rather embarrassed.

Sue laughed. "Don't worry, Maggie. I know he can be extremely difficult at times."

"Incidentally," said Maggie, trying to sound casual, "what do you know about Jutta Volk? I came across a book by her in the Taylorian. I get the impression that she's not all that popular in certain quarters."

Sue looked at her thoughtfully and sipped her sherry. "No, she's not," she said slowly. "And particularly not with Nicholas, as you probably gathered when we were all together."

"What do you know about her?" asked Maggie, thinking it might be better not to make any comment about that.

"Well, not a great deal about her relationship with Nicholas—that was before we knew him," Sue replied. "I don't think there was ever anything serious as far as he was concerned, but I believe Jutta was very smitten." She paused. "However, she must've got over it, because she became extremely friendly with Heike. I know Nicholas wasn't at all happy about that. I think he felt she had far too great an influence over her, particularly in persuading her that she should go to Jena to study."

Maggie stared into the fire as she digested this information. "And that was where Heike disappeared, was it?" she ventured.

"That's the strange thing," answered Sue reflectively, as she topped up Maggie's glass. "She was certainly based there at the beginning, but no one was able to give Nicholas any information when he went looking for her—it was as if she'd disappeared without trace. What made it more difficult for him was that it was the time when the Wall came down, and there was confusion everywhere."

"He must've been devastated—not knowing," Maggie said.

"I think he was—is—though now, I think in his heart of hearts, he's really given up hope of her ever coming back." Sue looked straight at Maggie as she continued, "To be frank, I think this is why he's rather moody sometimes."

Not just sometimes, thought Maggie, but didn't dare say so.

"The problem is, he can't really handle another person he loves disappearing." Sue got up to put another log on the fire.

"You mean this has happened to him before," said Maggie wide-eyed.

Sue looked at her for a moment before replying, "What I'm about to tell you is strictly between us, Maggie, okay? Nicholas is a very private person, and I wouldn't like this to go any further." After Maggie had given her word, Sue paused to collect her thoughts before continuing slowly, choosing her words with care "Nicholas had a very troubled childhood—he was born in St Petersburg in the 1930s when Stalin's purges were at their height. His father was a writer of children's books, and by the mid-30s, he and others like him were being referred to as counterrevolutionary and enemies of the state. One night, there was a pounding at their front door, and Nicholas has vivid memories of his mother's screams and his father's cries of pain as he was beaten by his captors and dragged away. He's told us that he recalls his mother's face wet with tears as she came to him and gathered him and his baby sister in her arms. His father was never seen again, though Nicholas discovered later that he'd been deported to a labour camp in Siberia." Sue paused. "Now, perhaps, you can understand why Heike's disappearance seemed almost like a repeat of his childhood experience."

"What a dreadful story!" Maggie exclaimed. "Whatever did his mother do? She had two young children. She must've been so afraid."

"Well, she was." Sue continued, "Particularly as she was a curator at the Hermitage and many of her colleagues were being shot as spies. Nicholas was never able to discover why she didn't try and escape to England, which she could've done as she was half English and had relatives there. But by the summer of 1941, it was too late, because the Germans were beginning to surround Leningrad, as it was then called, and people became more intent on survival. Also, his mother was involved in helping to save the treasures in the Hermitage. Nicholas remembers working with her as she packed small paintings and precious jewellery into large wooden crates so they could be taken away by train to a safer place. Nicholas has never spoken to us about the siege—it went on for 900 days, you know—I think the memories of it are still too painful, though he has mentioned the cold, gnawing hunger and bodies everywhere in the streets."

Maggie gazed at Sue as she finished speaking, and there was a long silence as she absorbed what she'd just been told. "Thank you for telling me all this," she said quietly. "I promise I'll keep it all to myself. I think I understand things a lot better now."

"I'm glad," replied Sue. "That was one of the reasons I wanted to tell you." She got up. "Another sherry, Maggie?"

Maggie glanced at her watch, and to her horror, saw that it was gone 7 p.m. "Thanks, Sue, but no. I really must be getting back to the farm. I've got a lot of preparation to do for tomorrow. Thank you very much, again, for everything."

"Why don't you come over for supper on Saturday?" suggested Sue as she showed her out. "I know John would like to meet you again."

Maggie's face brightened. "I'd love to, thanks."

"Good—that's settled then," said Sue. "See you about 7 p.m.," and she waved her off. *Hm*, she thought to herself reflectively as she shut the front door, *I think I'll see if Nicholas is free next Saturday.*

Chapter 11

Heike didn't know what to expect when she arrived at Lotte's house late that afternoon, carrying a bunch of flowers for her hostess. After her initial enthusiasm the day before, she was wondering if she'd made the right decision in accepting this invitation and whether the surveillance she was now having to put up with would become more marked because she was visiting someone in Jena. Unusual actions often bred suspicion, with so many informers spying on others.

She glanced round to see if anyone was following her as she left her apartment. It was an instinctive gesture, and she felt stupid for doing it. "Don't let them get you down," she told herself. "Just get on with your life as if they weren't there; otherwise, they've won."

This was easier said than done, though, and as Heike started walking down Goethestrasse, she really had to fight the temptation to glance across the street towards the waiting car, still in its customary position with its watchful occupants lurking behind the darkened windows.

When she arrived in Torgasse, there was a cool wind blowing straight down the narrow little street, but the pale, early autumn sun was shining on the old façade, and Lotte's house looked a lot more welcoming than it had on her last visit. At least, this time, she also had the comfort of knowing she was expected, and no sooner had she knocked than she heard shuffling footsteps and the door creaked slowly open—only a crack at first to allow the occupant a chance to check up on her visitor. Then, when she was satisfied that all was well, the door was swung a little wider, allowing Heike her first glimpse of Jutta's old tutor.

The face that peered out at her seemed to Heike like a little brown bird—a thin, bony face with a beak of a nose and small bright eyes that appeared to be assessing her in some way. But she was welcoming enough and ushered Heike into a small sitting room lined with books, where a cheerful fire was burning in a blackened stove that had obviously seen a lot of use. Heike sat down beside the fire where her hostess had indicated, gratefully stretching her cold fingers towards the welcome blaze.

Lotte, meanwhile, bustled about, setting out the tea on a table near the fire. Considering the austerity of the times, there was a considerable amount of food, and Heike wondered idly how Lotte had afforded the varied types of bread and beautiful gateaux that had obviously been bought from a black-market source. It was all served on exquisite fragile porcelain, and Heike would have been enjoying this unexpected luxury very much, had she not sensed that Lotte was visibly nervous and noted that her hand shook a little as she placed Heike's cup and plate on a little table beside her. In some sense, too, Heike felt that she was being observed, not just by Lotte as she sat opposite her by the fire, but by some unseen watcher.

However, their conversation at first seemed innocuous enough. Lotte asked for up-to-date news of Jutta and wanted to know how Heike's research was going. Heike explained exactly what she was trying to do, while Lotte nodded wisely from time to time. She also asked Heike about Nicholas and her life in Oxford and surprisingly seemed to be quite familiar with Heike's background. Heike wondered a little at the extent of her knowledge, but thought to herself that this had probably all come via Jutta. She was never quite sure how this happened, but she found herself being questioned closely about her political beliefs and what she thought about the recent demonstrations in Leipzig and whether she had ever been to the Monday prayer meetings and joined in the protests outside the Nikolaikirche. Heike felt that she was being pumped for information and tested in some way and was unsure as to what she should be saying.

"I haven't had much time for travelling around," she mumbled in the end. "It's been such a short time, and I've had a lot to do… just getting used to the university life here and making progress on my research."

Lotte nodded and appeared satisfied with her response, but something about the way she was being questioned sent a chill down Heike's spine. Why was Lotte asking her all these things? What was she trying to find out? She felt suddenly on her guard and shifted uneasily in her chair.

"They're trying to bring our government down, you know—them and that Mikhail Gorbachev," burst out Lotte suddenly, her face flushed with anger. Then, seeing Heike's puzzled expression, she continued, "He's been over here, telling Mielke and Honecker he's withdrawing Russian support for our country.

It'll mean the end for us and our little country after forty years struggling against the plots of the fascist capitalists in the west."

Heike looked at her, rather perplexed. For a little old, retired lady, this all seemed rather unexpected. Lotte was looking at her expectantly, and Heike felt she had to say something in reply.

"Well," she ventured in the end, remembering Nicholas's argument, "Gorbachev is only suggesting economic reform and more openness of speech."

"That may be so," countered Lotte, her brown, beady eyes glowing with fervour, "but without Soviet military support, we can't survive at the moment. Only a short time ago, Hungary cut its border with Austria, and this has made a hole in the eastern bloc defences. It's the beginning of the end if we don't do something about it."

"I don't see what we can do," she objected. Despite herself though, she couldn't help being moved by Lotte's strength of feeling. Lotte's words had also stirred up old hidden emotions deep down in her own subconsciousness— nationalistic emotions that she had never been able to fully share with Nicholas or anyone else since her parents had died. If she had even hinted at them, it had raised past resentment and anguish that he still laid at the door of her country, she knew. Nationalism was definitely not something that the Germans openly mentioned.

"We must and we will," continued Lotte with the same fervour, "and these demonstrations are not helping. You don't want to see East Germany disappear, do you?"

Heike thought long and hard. To tell the truth, she was not sure what she wanted. She and Nicholas had argued so many times over this issue—he held more liberal views than she did, perhaps. Though, was this because he didn't like Germany, whether East or West? That might mean he was indifferent to what happened—that he might like to see a weakened Germany. She realised Lotte was watching her keenly.

"You're researching Christa Wolf, aren't you?" she said. "And she's all for two separate countries, with East Germany representing the true face of socialism."

"Yes, but with a reformed government here," countered Heike.

"Certainly," agreed Lotte. "That's what I'd like to see, too, but to buy time for that, we need a more hardline Russian leader to support us for a bit longer while we try to bring about reforms here."

"But how can we possibly change Russian policy?" said Heike incredulously. "They hold all the cards."

Lotte didn't answer her question directly but paused a moment and looked closely at Heike. "You're an East German, my dear. Do you want to lose your identity, your Heimat, your sense of belonging? We, all of us, need to feel deep down that we are part of a community. Do you feel that in England?"

Despite Heike's initial reserve and unease, she found herself being drawn to this elderly lady speaking so passionately about her own country. Although she'd been living in the UK for many years, she certainly didn't feel that she belonged—particularly now that she'd lost both her parents. As an immigrant, perhaps, you never really feel you are a part of the host country, however welcoming it may be. You lose your language and your culture and are, in many ways, displaced. "Did Nicholas feel the same?" she wondered. She realised that Lotte had struck a chord within her that was only now really coming to the surface—perhaps that was why she had so wanted to come to Jena and had risked her relationship with Nicholas to do so.

Lotte, seeing the doubt and uncertainty in her face, wisely decided to say no more, but instead, offered Heike more tea and another slice of delicious gateau. When Heike finally got up to leave, Lotte kissed her warmly on both cheeks and invited her to come again the following week.

"I've so enjoyed our conversation, my dear," she said, "and I do get a little lonely these days." As the front door closed behind Heike, Lotte re-entered the sitting room and turning towards the half-open door of the dining room, asked nervously, "How do you think that went?"

* * * * *

The light was fading as Heike walked briskly down Torgasse. Their conversation had been so absorbing that she hadn't realised how long she'd been with Lotte. She was so deep in thought after her visit that she failed to notice the car following her until she got to St Michaelis, Jena's parish church. It was a white Wartburg with darkened windows, and although it was virtually dark by this time, the lights were turned off as it drew nearer to her. She nervously quickened her step as she crossed the Marktplatz, but the unknown driver just kept pace with her.

Heike had heard many stories of the Stasi snatching people off the street, and they were never heard of again. Really fearful now, she broke into a breathless run until she got to the nearby Muhlgasschen—a covered alleyway, too narrow for the car to follow her. She was mightily relieved to see no sign of it when she left the relative security of that little street. Although she continued to hurry along at some speed, she was now unsure as to whether it was safe for her to go back to the apartment. However, as the temperature dropped, and light but persistent rain began to fall, she didn't have any other option.

She felt a little safer when she neared Goethestrasse, as the streets were now more crowded with others hurrying home as she was. She stopped in a doorway and looked carefully around but couldn't see the white car anywhere—even the space usually occupied by the black Trabant was empty, though this often happened in the evenings. She quickly unlocked the door into the apartment block and, shutting it behind her, stood in the darkened hallway with heart thumping and tears running down her face. When she reached the security of her own apartment, she locked the door and made a careful search—but all was just as she'd left it. She began to breathe more easily, though she became aware that she was trembling all over.

With shaking hands, she opened the vodka she had bought at the airport for Nicholas. It was the only alcohol she had in the flat, and she was certainly not going out on the streets again that night. A couple of glasses later, she began to feel steadier and tried to rationalise to herself what had just happened. The Stasi often escalated their surveillance for no real reason except to increase the pressure on their victim. After all, they could have picked her off the deserted streets around the square any time if they'd seriously intended to harm her. The fact they hadn't done so had to mean she was low priority as far as they were concerned.

Heike would've liked to have phoned Nicholas for reassurance, just to hear the sound of his familiar voice, but the connection wasn't always easily made, and she was almost certain that her phone was being tapped. This frequently happened to newcomers or those the authorities weren't certain of. No, better not; it wasn't the time to be making sensitive calls. Another quick peep out of her window revealed neither black Trabant or white Wartburg, and because she was beginning to feel rather light-headed after the vodka, she decided she'd better have something to eat.

Just as she was sitting down to her meal, the telephone rang. Heike stiffened and felt a cold chill at the pit of her stomach. She was of half a mind to ignore it but then knew that she'd spend the rest of the evening wondering who had tried to call her. Her voice sounded quavery even to herself as she answered, but to her relief, it was only Marta, reminding her rather curtly about a lecture on Monday morning. Heike sighed as she replaced the receiver and felt rather friendless and alone. The only person who had really made her welcome had been Lotte. *She was quite a dear old thing*, she thought, and her visit there had certainly been thought provoking. She remembered Lotte's bitter remarks about the demonstrations in Leipzig. It had made her curious to know more.

"I wonder whether I should go to one of the Monday evening prayer meetings at the Nicholaikirche, just to see what it's like," she mused as she finished her supper. "It's obviously become a real focus for the demonstrators, and I might even get to chat to some of them. That could be really interesting."

She realised that by going there, she might draw further attention to herself as far as the Stasi were concerned.

"It could be dangerous, I suppose," she said to herself as she washed up her supper things. "Perhaps, I'm a bit stupid even to think of it."

This time, they had really got to her and found a weak point. Unconsciously, she tightened her lips and felt a steely determination not to be browbeaten by them and decided, after thinking about it a bit more, to go to Leipzig after her lecture. She went to bed buoyed up by that decision and hoped she'd still feel as brave in the morning.

Chapter 12

Despite John's dire predictions, Sue's supper party turned out to be a great success.

"This could be a total disaster," he warned her when he heard what she'd done. "You should've said something to Nicholas when you invited him. He might just turn around and go home when he finds Maggie here."

"He mightn't have come at all then," Sue said defensively. She was certainly not going to admit she was feeling a bit apprehensive herself now. "And I'm sure he'll enjoy himself once he gets here."

"I'd better get plenty of drinks organised," he said as he stomped off, looking unconvinced.

Though she was initially startled when Nicholas arrived, Maggie visibly relaxed in his company as the evening wore on, due in part to the Wintertons' generous hospitality. And Nicholas didn't look at all displeased to see Maggie, Sue was relieved to see. In fact, he looked at her rather appreciatively as she stammered an awkward "Hello" from her seat by the fire when he entered the sitting room. Her silvery cashmere sweater and black silk trousers were casual but elegant, and her fair hair and lightly tanned skin glowed from the warmth of the fire. Though Maggie managed adroitly to avoid the use of his Christian name, she and Nicholas were so obviously enjoying each other's company that Sue decided to leave them well alone. They seemed to have a lot in common as they chatted about skiing and Russian history, which Maggie seemed as passionate about as Nicholas.

"Why are you so interested in Russia, Maggie?" John asked her curiously while they were having dinner.

"That's hard to explain," she said thoughtfully. "It's just that Russian music and literature have always fascinated me, and I stayed there for several months so that I could learn the language." Her face lit up with enthusiasm as she described Russian cultural achievements in the eighteenth century and how talented a race they were.

Sue glanced at Nicholas and noted the intent look on his face while Maggie was speaking. Maggie broke off in confusion as she became aware that he was watching her, and despite all of Sue's endeavours, refused to be drawn further. However, she'd regained her confidence enough by the time the dessert came round to argue with Nicholas about the music of Shostakovich. He quickly realised that she was extremely knowledgeable about this great Russian composer and had obviously made quite a study of his life and work. When Maggie described the impact of the performance of his seventh symphony in a besieged Leningrad in 1942, she unknowingly touched a chord as Nicholas recalled attending that incredible performance with his mother and seeing tears running down her face.

"There are many Russians who don't know as much as you do about my country. You're a very knowledgeable person, Maggie," he said quietly when she'd finished speaking. Maggie blushed at this rare praise.

While Sue was pouring out their coffee as they sat round the fire again, he watched Maggie as she chatted to John. She radiated a sense of inner tranquillity and an aura of calm that was very restful, he thought. She was so different from Heike, who had so often appeared anxious and on the defensive.

"You seem to be very happy and at ease with your life here in Oxford, Maggie," he said suddenly.

Maggie was startled by the unexpectedness of his remark and spoke without thinking, "You wouldn't think that if you could see me sometimes tearing my hair out over some assignment a crusty old professor has set me." She stopped, aghast, realising what she had just said. In the awkward pause that followed, she bit her lip, aware that she had been betrayed into an indiscretion in this relaxing atmosphere. "I'm so sorry," she stammered. "I wasn't referring to you, of course."

To her relief, Nicholas chuckled, and Sue, seeing Maggie's discomfiture, said quickly, "Well, it would serve him right if you did mean Nicholas. I'm sure he can be very crusty at times." In the ensuing laughter, Maggie relaxed again as she realised that she'd not really put her foot in it and that Nicholas had clearly enjoyed her frank assessment of Oxford professors.

The conversation continued to flow so effortlessly among the four of them that it was the early hours before Nicholas and Maggie took their leave. Nicholas kissed his hostess on both cheeks, thanking her profusely for a splendid evening and as he turned towards Maggie, he unthinkingly also kissed her goodbye. Then overcome with embarrassment when he realised what he had done, he mumbled a hurried "Goodnight," before disappearing down the garden path. Fortunately for Maggie, the darkness hid her confusion as she, too, thanked both Sue and John for a wonderful evening.

"Well," said Sue triumphantly to John as she closed the front door, "what did you think of that?"

She would have felt even more triumphant if she'd been able to read Nicholas's thoughts as he stood in the middle of his quiet sitting room, pondering over the evening he'd just spent. He realised that this was the first time he'd really felt drawn to another woman since Heike's disappearance. His doubts about Heike and what she'd been up to were mingled with a sense of guilt and disloyalty, but he was also aware that, almost against his will, the memory of her was not as strong as before and that his bitter longing and unhappiness were being replaced by an inner contentment. These feelings of contentment didn't last, however, and were replaced by further pangs of guilt that he should even consider fancying anyone else when he didn't know for sure that Heike had done anything wrong or if she was even dead. The letter he'd received so many months ago might have been totally untrue.

As he made his way upstairs, these bouts of self-recrimination were mingled with the realisation that as Maggie's supervisor, he couldn't possibly consider any relationship with her, however platonic. Oxford was a hotbed of gossip, and he certainly didn't want to imperil Maggie's chances of a degree by any whisper of favouritism on his part. He determined that there would be no more cosy supper parties and warned Sue kindly but firmly when he next met her, not to set up any other surprise invitations throwing him and Maggie together. Her face showed her disappointment, but he told her gently that it just wouldn't do. When she tried to suggest that he ought to develop a new life now and come to terms with the loss of Heike, he said rather stiffly that he hadn't given up searching for her and would probably go back to Jena during the long summer vacation. With a sigh of resignation, Sue realised there was no point in pressing him further.

Despite having made this decision, he felt tense when Maggie arrived for her usual tutorial the week following the supper party. He made every effort to be professional and detached, but there was a feeling of constraint between them. For her part, Maggie felt unsure as to how he would be after the informality of their last meeting, and Nicholas, to his dismay, couldn't conceal from himself how pleased he was to see her and tried to hide this by a stiff formality.

Fortunately, these sessions together were now more infrequent than the previous term, as Maggie was having to focus much more on the philosophical content of her degree. Preoccupations about this were so much on her mind that it left little room for concerns about a good working relationship with her supervisor. She would soon be presenting her seminar and worried about this and whether she was going to make a complete fool of herself, so occupied her mind that she had little time for any other problems. Sebastian was proving a tower of strength, providing a sympathetic ear when needed, and firmly insisting on taking her to concerts on a regular basis and then out for a pizza. She had come to rely on his friendship, though the growing warmth in his manner sometimes bothered her.

On one occasion, while working in the college library in her usual 'nest', she'd felt herself being observed. On looking up, she had seen Sebastian at a neighbouring table, his gaze fixed on her. He had flushed when he realised that she had spotted him and had bent his head quickly over his book, and it had troubled her a little. He was ten years younger than her, and she certainly didn't want any romantic entanglements to spoil the ease of their relationship.

The day before her seminar presentation, he suggested going to the Holywell Music Room for a change, and they arranged to meet there. Maggie had never been inside this lovely old building before and was surprised to see every seat was taken.

"I've passed it so many times and never guessed how popular it was," she said when she joined Sebastian.

"It has a very faithful following," he replied as they sat down. "It's a really good venue for chamber concerts, and although it's small, it has marvellous acoustics."

"It's just a pity that the inside hasn't been decorated to match the beautiful façade," grimaced Maggie, looking at the rather shabby paintwork.

"Everyone who comes here wants that," agreed Sebastian, "The problem is getting Wadham College to agree!"

Maggie laughed. "Changes take a long time to achieve in Oxford."

As they settled themselves in their seats, Sue turned to speak to Nicholas and saw him staring across the hall to where Sebastian and Maggie were sitting. Sebastian was obviously telling some story and she was smiling up at him. Sue noticed how a rigid expression came over Nicholas's face, and his jaw hardened. He was unusually quiet the whole evening, and when they returned home, turned down John's offer of a nightcap. Sue opened her mouth to speak, but John put a restraining hand on her arm and shook his head. They heard his front door slam violently behind him.

Chapter 13

Most of the group were already gathered round the long oval table when Maggie got to the seminar room at St John's. Her mouth was really dry from nerves as she put her carefully prepared manuscript in front of one of the spare seats. She knew she only had to read it out, but delivery was everything, and then there were the questions at the end. Professor Cooper would be listening carefully, she knew, and probably taking notes, because this would form part of her final examination mark. When Professor Cooper came in, everyone quickly found their places. Maggie sat down, making sure that the pages of her presentation were in order and praying that her voice wouldn't quaver as she started and that her hands wouldn't shake. Professor Cooper nodded kindly in her direction and asked her to begin when she was ready.

Afterwards, she couldn't have said whether she'd read it correctly or not and whether it had gone down well, but when she laid her papers down, everyone seemed quite interested in what she'd had to say. The one or two questions that followed appeared to indicate that some had been listening, anyway. Professor Cooper made no comment, but then, he hadn't done so for the other presentations either, so that wasn't going to worry her too much. She only realised how nervous and wound up she'd been at the prospect of this seminar when she was walking back up along St Giles in the gathering dusk. She suddenly felt desperately tired and decided to pop into the nearest wine store, buy a bottle of wine and go straight back to the caravan. Oxford, she realised for the umpteenth time, could be an extremely stressful place.

The next day, rested and refreshed, though with a sense of anti-climax, she went into collage on her usual bus. She had an assignment to do for Professor Stowkovsky before the end of term, and she had a lot of reading to do. Her 'nest' looked welcoming and undisturbed, and Maggie had just settled down when Angie arrived. In a stage whisper, she indicated that she needed to talk to her urgently. With a sigh, Maggie followed her out of the library and down to the JCR which, for once, was completely empty. Angie brought over two cups of coffee and then broke the news that she was having an affair with a tutor in one of the other colleges. Actually, Maggie had had her suspicions for some time but hadn't wanted to say anything. She knew that Angie was married—in fact, she had met her husband Philip and their three children at a college function—and she certainly didn't want to get involved in her friend's extramarital relationships.

"Why are you telling me?" she asked rather warily. "You need to keep this as quiet as possible."

"I know, I know," said Angie tearfully, "but we were spotted by some students, and even worse, by the principal's secretary the other night."

"Whatever were you up to? You weren't…"

"No, nothing like that," Angie broke in hastily. "I'm not that stupid. We were just kissing outside his college. I'm now really worried that the news is going to leak out."

Maggie decided there was no point in telling her what a fool she'd been, behaving so indiscreetly. She could see that Angie was genuinely worried and close to tears. She couldn't really think of what to say except to advise the two of them to stop seeing one another. Angie sniffed into her handkerchief and agreed, though not very convincingly, and Maggie left her drowning her sorrows in another cup of coffee and wondered what her mercurial friend would get up to next.

As she sat down again in the library, she now found it hard to settle down to work. Her thoughts inexplicably drifted back to her last tutorial. She couldn't hide from herself the fact that there had been a strained atmosphere and that if it had been anyone other than Professor Stowkovsky, she would have felt there'd been an element of sexual tension. Yet, this seemed a very unlikely scenario. At times, he was so abrupt with her, it was almost as if he resented her presence in some way, while on the other hand, when he was relaxed, his manner was warm and friendly, and he visibly appeared to enjoy her company. He was so unpredictable. She sighed, thinking how hard it was to gauge what he really thought of her or her work, his manner during their last meeting had been almost frosty.

Maggie looked down at her hands and realised she was twisting her wedding ring to and fro. It was an old habit, and she always did it when she was preoccupied. She sighed again. Tim had placed it there on their wedding day nearly thirty years ago. As a naval surgeon, he had travelled out to the South

Atlantic at the start of the Falklands War and had been one of the early causalities. Maggie had slowly and painfully come to terms with this loss and thrown herself heart and soul into her career at a Further Education College, teaching English to foreign students. She had carved out a very pleasant life with a comfortable flat in London and a wide circle of friends. She was an inveterate traveller and made use of the long summer vacations, visiting her many friends and relatives in different parts of the world.

Yet, despite her best efforts to suppress it, she sometimes felt the pang of loss of what might have been. It was as if with all that activity, she was running away from something or searching for a meaning to her life. Perhaps, that was why she had decided to do this degree and that it was giving a focus to her life. What had she been looking for when she came to Oxford? Perhaps an answer to the rest of her life. Perhaps a chance to develop a new self-awareness, a fresh confidence. Though at the moment her self-confidence was at a low ebb. One or two chairs scraping on the oak floor as students got up to leave the library jerked her out of her reverie. She looked at the library clock and saw to her horror that it was already time to go over for lunch. With a sense of panic, she realised that she had wasted the whole morning and achieved absolutely nothing.

The remainder of the Hilary Term was occupied with not only with Maggie's own emotional problems but also those of her friends. Angie's affair with her lecturer friend Tom from St Cross leaked out, as was inevitable, and there were whispers that Tom's wife was going to sue for divorce and cite Angie as the woman responsible for the break-up of her marriage. Angie, white-faced with dark shadows under her eyes, sought out Maggie as a reliable shoulder to cry on. Anna, a Russian friend from the philosophy group, received bad news from home that her mother had just been diagnosed with stomach cancer, and Maggie found her weeping quietly to herself in the gardens at St John's just before her seminar presentation. To make matters worse, Sebastian proposed to Maggie as they walked down to the river one Saturday afternoon. Maggie, completely taken aback by the violence of his emotion when she gently told him that she couldn't accept, could only watch helplessly as he angrily strode away from her, nearly knocking down a mother with her child in his agitation.

Maggie knew that their friendship on which she had come to rely could not survive and walked back to college in very low spirits indeed. She didn't see him for several days, but when their paths finally crossed, he averted his eyes and hurried past her with only a brief muffled greeting. Her sessions with her supervisor were as highly charged as ever, though at least the grades she was receiving for her work were now consistently in the 60s. After her last tutorial of the term, she came away with a sense of relief that she now had some weeks of vacation to recover from what had proved to be a very stressful term indeed.

Chapter 14

Maggie took the steep stairs two at a time. She knew she was late, and Nicholas Stowkovsky was a stickler as far as punctuality was concerned. Yet again, Angie had waylaid her with more problems in her complicated love life, and she had been unable to shake her off and was too kind-hearted to simply tell her that she hadn't got time to listen. After she had grabbed her books and papers from her locker, Maggie had run all the way from college at breakneck speed and, heedless of the traffic, had charged across Broad Street, risking life and limb as she dodged between cars and bicycles, leaving in her wake an angry hooting of horns and some flustered cyclists. She did a final sprint down Turl Street and a quick glance at her watch showed to her horror that she was at least a quarter of an hour late. Her fair hair was tousled, she knew, but there was no time to stop and put a comb through it. *Damn Angie*, she thought as she arrived panting at her supervisor's door. She had so wanted to arrive for this particular tutorial appearing calm and collected as if she were fully in control of her life. Instead of which, she knew she was looking pink and flurried and very disorganised.

She wasn't looking forward to this session with Professor Stowkovsky because she now had to come to a decision about her dissertation subject, and she realised that she should have put much more time into thinking about it. There seemed to have been so many other things occupying her mind, but it was now the third week of Trinity Term, and her topic had to be submitted to the Graduate Studies Assistant by next week at the latest, so it was getting a bit urgent. The problem was that she'd rather lost interest in her original topic focussing on the role of the narrator in some of Tolstoy's work.

For some time, she'd felt she'd much rather do a comparative study between Russian and East German writers. She had been dreading telling her supervisor this. He always became irritable when she suggested doing work along these lines. The Easter break had provided an opportunity to think about what she really wanted to do, and she was also now wondering whether to ask for a change of supervisor next year. The relationship between her and Nicholas seemed so difficult. There was a certain tension in the air that she couldn't quite understand, and she was finding difficult to handle. He was so edgy with her and so unpredictable. But she was unsure who to discuss this with. Angie was too preoccupied with her own worries to be of any use and Sebastian hardly spoke to her now. She felt that she could hardly talk to her supervisor about how concerned she was.

She knocked timidly on his door and waited nervously for him to answer. When she entered, she noticed that instead of sitting at his desk as normal, he was standing by the window, as if deep in thought. As he turned and gestured that she should sit down, her heart sank. From the look on his face, he was obviously in one of his moods. To hide her nervousness, Maggie busied herself with laying out her papers on which she had scribbled some notes about the new topic she wanted to do.

"You're late," he said curtly and waved aside her stumbled apology as he sat down opposite her. "We have important matters to discuss today, and I have other students to see."

The moment he uttered these words, Nicholas hated himself for speaking so abruptly to Maggie but hoped that his harsh tone might conceal his inner turmoil. Before her arrival, he had been struggling with his usual feelings of guilt about Heike and a sense that he was betraying her by even thinking of another woman. Yet, did he owe her anything? He thought back to that letter that had arrived so many months ago and was still stuffed in his desk drawer. If it was to be believed, it was she who had perhaps betrayed him, and anyway, she might well be dead, for all he knew. Among these confused emotions, he also realised that the powerful attraction he was beginning to feel for Maggie was growing, as was the jealousy of any man who was free to take her out. Though he fought against it, he was aware that he was spending far too much time thinking about her. He even found himself looking out for her as he made his way through the Oxford streets. He would scan the bent heads of the students working in the Bodleian or Taylorian hoping for a glimpse of her.

"You're behaving like a lovesick boy," he told himself. "This just won't do."

Because much as he wanted to, he knew that he could not make any move towards her that would involve them both in a scandal. He had heard the rumours in the SCR about an affair between Dr Tom Jackson and Angie Houghton, and he was only too aware what gossip like that would do not only to his reputation but also to Maggie's prospects of a good degree next year. And then, there was the search for Heike, which he was now planning for the summer vacation. Was he going to abandon this? It would be like a final abandonment of her as his wife, when he wasn't even sure what she'd been up to in Germany or whether she was dead or alive. He only had the word of that unknown letter-writer. Was he going to desert her as he felt he had deserted his mother all those years ago in Leningrad? Waiting for Maggie to arrive for her tutorial, all these thoughts were racing through his mind as he paced up and down his study. He cast his mind back to those dreadful days of the Leningrad siege that even now, he could hardly bear to talk about, and had tried unsuccessfully to put out of his mind.

For 900 days, the people of Leningrad had struggled and starved and died in that unbearable time between 1941 and 1944 until the Red Army drove the Germans through eastern Europe as far as Berlin. Nicholas remembered the constant gnawing hunger in his stomach as the daily bread ration continued to be drastically reduced to a mere small handful. His mother, her face gaunt and emaciated, did her best to feed her little family. By the end of that first dreadful winter, she was even using her face powder for flour and melting her lipstick to fry bread. All their books were put on their stove, but the temperature in their home never rose above freezing as they sat huddled round the tiny fire in all their clothes.

He recalled going out with his mother to get their bread ration clutching their precious ration cards and seeing people like ghosts moving through the snow and ice often pulling a children's sled on which lay a dead body wrapped in a sheet or someone leaning against a wall too exhausted to walk. Frozen bodies lay in the snow where those too weak to continue had simply collapsed and died. The following summer of 1942 brought some relief, and like so many others, Nicholas and his mother and baby sister planted vegetables in a little garden to plan for the winter to come. It was around this time that his mother started fretting about not having sent Nicholas and Alexandra away to safety with the other children before the blockade had begun.

"We might not survive another winter," Nicholas heard her say to a neighbour. "I should have done more to save my babies."

A myriad of images flashed through his mind as he strode up and down, occasionally running his fingers through his hair, once dark and now streaked liberally with grey. That concert in the Philharmonic Hall in the summer of 1942 was one of the better memories. Though still in the German grip, the people of

Leningrad flocked to hear their orchestra play Shostakovich's 7th Symphony, music that so symbolised their struggle. Nicholas saw his mother weeping silently as she remembered her husband far away—perhaps not even alive. It was as if this concert was a catalyst, because as soon as the direct rail connection with the rest of Russia reopened, she insisted that Nicholas and Alexandra should make the journey to Moscow with another family. From there, as soon as it was practicable, they were to travel to Scotland to stay with her sister. In vain, Nicholas protested that he was now head of the family and should be taking care of her.

His mother was firm. "I shall have work to do here, Nicholas. After all, our Hermitage treasures return to St Petersburg, but when it's safe to do so, you can both come home."

His last memory of his mother was her shrunken figure waving goodbye at the station. His eyes blurred with tears, he waved till he could see her no more. That was the final time he saw her, and he never lost the feeling that he had abandoned her and that perhaps, she would still be alive today if he had stayed with her.

Maggie's knock had broken into these black thoughts that were once again tormenting him. As he looked at her, he felt love and hate in equal measure. These complex emotions mingled with the knowledge that he was in charge of her studies and had a responsibility to ensure that she had every chance of being successful. He noticed the alarm in her grey eyes and felt a pang of conscience that he was making her unhappy. He noted her trembling fingers as she laid her papers out on his desk and wanted to reach out and touch her hand in reassurance. There was within him this longing to see her, this aching to touch her, yet in a strange way a resentment of these feelings.

"Right, Maggie," he continued in what he hoped was as normal a manner as possible, "let us now discuss your dissertation title for next year."

As Maggie had feared, he was not at all happy with her change of topic, and when she persisted, he stood up and suggested coldly that she should go away and think again about what she wanted to do. Maggie, who by now was both angry and upset, got up to leave, and without thinking, blurted out that she not only wanted to change her topic but also her supervisor.

There was a moment's terrible silence until Maggie, half-afraid at what she had just said stammered, "I'm sorry, I didn't mean…"

The words were only half-uttered when Nicholas, without warning, took two steps towards her, seized her arms and pulled her towards him with such force that the books she was holding fell to the floor. For a moment, he held her close to him, his fingers biting into her arms, his eyes blazing, hers bewildered and frightened. As she cried out in pain, he kissed her harshly for only a second before thrusting her away from him. Maggie half fell against the desk, scattering books and papers. Then, heedless of the possessions she had dropped, she snatched her handbag and half-sobbing, ran from his study. Nicholas stared for a moment at the partly open door before slamming his fist so hard on the desk than blood ran from his grazed knuckles. He stared across the room to where his wife's photograph stood on the bookcase. He took one stride across the floor and seized the frame, flinging it at the opposite wall. The shards of glass scattered across the carpet and the photograph, still intact, lay amidst the debris, his wife's face smiling up at him.

Chapter 15

The myriad of twinkling candles wound its way like a snake through the narrow streets leading from the Nicholaikirche to the Runde Ecke where the demonstrators stood protesting outside the Stasi headquarters.

"No violence, no violence," some in the crowd called out as they shielded their candles from the wind that swirled around the sinister, grey stone building towering above them. The guards watched impassively as their cries grew louder and their numbers increased.

"We want democracy, we want democracy," a group shouted from the back of the crowd.

"We want freedom to travel," others yelled out in the ever-growing throng. Their brave chants reverberated around the silent, menacing facade. No one had ever been able to hear the screams of those unfortunate enough to be incarcerated there. The windows to their cells had been bricked in. But the few who had been fortunate enough to be released told of the dreadful scenes they had witnessed, the blood spattered walls and the broken bodies. The sight of the building alone normally made people shudder and cross the street. Those protesting knew that they were risking their lives but took comfort from the sheer weight of numbers and the lack of response by the authorities, normally so quick to react to any sign of rebellion by their citizens.

Heike, who had taken a candle from the church with the rest of the congregation, joined the procession. She shivered in the cool evening air, partly from excitement and anticipation of the demonstration that lay ahead and partly through some nameless fear that she might be marked out in some way.

The evening service in the old church had been very moving. While she was sitting there, she looked around at the beautiful classical interior, pale pink and green with white wooden pews and rich gold gilding. The ceiling was supported by enormous, fluted columns like giant palms spreading out over their heads. The fervent chants of the worshippers echoed through the white gated pews high above Heike's head, joining the green palm leaves as their voices rose into the vastness of the pale vaulted roofing of this lovely old church that had become the centre for all the protesters. After the prayers for peace, the congregation filed out.

Heike was not only amazed by the quiet determination of these ordinary people, both young and old, but also by the numbers—more than 2000 people leaving the church were welcomed by several thousand waiting outside, and there must have been nearly 70,000 people by the time they finally reached the Runde Ecke. She knew enough to realise that these protesters were facing a considerable risk by allowing their defiant voices to be heard so close to the Stasi headquarters. She gazed up at the sinister building looming over her.

Back in England, she'd heard so many stories of what went on in its interrogation cells, but being there brought her face to face with reality. During their increasingly acrimonious arguments, Nicholas had referred to these places of detention as examples of the barbarity of the East German authorities and the punitive, restrictive nature of its system. He ignored Heike's bitter references to Stalin's atrocities. She had tried vainly to shut her mind to his accusations and had usually escaped to the peace and quiet of the garden. Now she was here and actually involved with the protest going on around her, she was faced with the reality of the situation. She realised that she could no longer hide from the truth.

This is the place where so-called suspects are bundled in to be interrogated, she thought to herself. *This is where they are often tortured and then perhaps never seen again. This is the centre which recruits countless 'eyes and ears' to spy on my fellow citizens, sometimes willingly but often under coercion, with threats to livelihood or to family members if there is a lack of cooperation.*

It occurred to Heike again that she, too, might be marked down as a threat to the East German state by her presence here. She glanced around rather fearfully at the thought, but no one seemed to be particularly interested in her enclosed as she was amongst so many others and she felt confident enough to chant with everyone else and to chat to some of those around her. What really surprised her was that not all of those she spoke to wanted an end to East Germany as an independent unit, but they desperately desired reform, a change of government, and in particular, freedom of movement.

Heike remembered Lotte's words and wondered if perhaps, the old lady might be right and that the sheer scale of these demonstrations and the momentum that was being created, rather than bringing about the much-needed reforms, might end up destroying the government and the country itself and perhaps lead to unification with West Germany and a victory for capitalism as Lotte had said.

I'm not really sure I want this, she thought to herself as she stood there with the ever-growing crowd, holding her still flickering candle. She feared that very real loss of her identity, and it seemed there were others who agreed with her.

She made her way back to Jena in a thoughtful mood. She walked to her apartment from the railway station, still mulling over what she had seen and heard. She was so absorbed in her own thoughts that she did not notice that the streets were dark and empty. It left her very exposed and vulnerable. Then she suddenly became aware of a car slowly approaching behind her. Her throat became constricted and her heartbeat quickened as she turned and recognised the same white Wartburg. Its headlights were turned off as before, and its speed increased as she broke into a half run, but there was nowhere for her to escape to this time.

After a few seconds, it drew up beside her, and both front and back doors opened quickly, trapping her between them. Half-sobbing with fear, Heike tried to squeeze past, but one of the occupants leapt out and grabbed her, putting a hand over her mouth to prevent her from calling out. She could not see who was holding her, but it was clearly a powerfully built man.

His guttural voice hissed into her ear, "You're mixing with the wrong company. Wherever you've come from, little red-haired lady, you'd better go back there if you know what's good for you." With that, he banged her head viciously against one of the car doors, and Heike felt blood streaming down her face. "Take note of what I've said, or next time, you won't be so lucky." He pushed her violently to the ground, got into the car, and it roared away. The whole incident had taken no more than a few seconds, but it had seemed like a lifetime to Heike as she scrambled painfully to her feet. She had hurt herself in her fall, and the wound in her head was bleeding profusely.

With shaking hands, she mopped at her face with a handkerchief and continued her walk home, her breath coming in painful gasps as she limped along the pavement. The few passers-by stared at her curiously before hurrying past with their gazes averted. It didn't do to get involved with other people's problems under the present climate. You might get drawn into something dangerous or unpleasant. Heike was not only thoroughly shaken by this nightmarish encounter, but that guttural voice had also puzzled and frightened her. She was certain that it was not East German.

"Russian, perhaps," she winced as she missed her footing and tripped against an uneven paving slab. "Whoever they were, they hadn't worried about using violence against me."

They had clearly been on the lookout for her, and she now realised that her movements were definitely being monitored. Though, why she was being targeted, she didn't know. She wondered whether it wouldn't be more sensible to take the advice so roughly given, and that perhaps, she should now throw in the towel and go back to Oxford and to safety, though a resolve deep within her urged her not to give into bullying tactics.

"I've got to make a stand, show them I'm not afraid," she announced to the empty street.

She was less sure, however, when she looked at her face in the bathroom mirror. Fortunately, she had met no one as she made her way up to her own apartment, because anyone seeing her under the harsh lights of the hallway would have received quite a shock. One side of her face was badly bruised and swollen, and there was a deep cut in her temple where a corner of the door had pierced the skin. She winced as she bathed it as best she could and put a dressing on it to contain the bleeding. Her head was buzzing, and she felt sick and dizzy. She made herself a hot drink and sat for a few minutes, considering her options. Heike lost count of time as she sat huddled in the one comfortable chair the apartment possessed with her still-shaking hands clasping the half-finished coffee. The violence had really frightened her, but she was still puzzling about the identity of the man who had attacked her.

Had the Stasi got two groups of people shadowing her? She wondered. It seemed unlikely she was important enough, but really, she told herself again, the sensible thing to do would be to return home. She was only halfway through the research she wanted to do, and there was an inner core of strength within Heike that made her reluctant to give it up. All these thoughts went round and round in her mind, making her head throb even more painfully.

Nicholas would only say he'd warned me what would happen, she thought as she rose stiffly from her chair. She didn't want to face his triumph of being right. She decided she would sleep on it and see how she felt in the morning.

The next day dawned bright and clear, and Heike thought again about her situation as she prepared her breakfast. A quick look in the mirror had shown that the bruises on her face could be hidden by brushing her auburn curls further forward, and with the addition of some carefully applied make-up, no one would notice anything untoward. She resolved to continue at least until the end of the week. She was going to visit Lotte again, then, and after that, she would reconsider what she should do. The rest of the week passed peacefully enough, and Heike made sure that she stayed on busy streets as she walked between the university and the apartment. Although she realised that she was risking reprisals if spotted on the Saturday she once again headed for Torgasse and was encouraged by the fact that there was no sign of the white Wartburg. Lotte had obviously been eagerly awaiting her and she opened the door the moment she knocked.

"I've really been looking forward to seeing you again, my dear," she said, kissing her warmly on both cheeks. "Come on in, tea's ready and we have lots to talk about."

Although Heike longed to pour out all her worries to such a sympathetic old lady and ask for her advice, some inner voice cautioned her not to mention her brutal attackers earlier that week. She'd already decided that it might also be more prudent not to mention her visit to Leipzig, so the conversation ranged over fairly innocuous subjects as she enjoyed the same sumptuous tea as before. It was not long, however, before Lotte asked her if she had had any further thoughts about their previous conversation.

"Yes, I have," said Heike cautiously, "and I can see there is a lot of sense in what you said—we do need to preserve our identity and not lose our sense of who we are. We could easily get swallowed up by West Germany."

"Exactly," said Lotte, her brown eyes shining. "I'm so glad you see it that way, my dear."

"But," objected Heike, "I hate the way the government treats those who disagree with the system, and I don't really see what we can do to prevent our country disappearing if things continue the way they're going."

"Ah," said Lotte getting up. "We've made a plan, but we need your help."

Before Heike could question her further, she made her way out into the hallway. Heike could hear her speaking to someone, and when she returned, she was accompanied by a thick-set, middle-aged man with such an obvious similarity to Lotte that Heike wasn't at all surprised when her hostess introduced him proudly as her son, Dietrich. He nodded briefly as he sat down with them round the fire. Lotte poured him out some tea, and as he took the cup, Heike felt a sense of unease. He sat there, silently drinking his tea and glancing at her from time to time, with a hard, expressionless gaze as if weighing her up in some way.

Lotte seemed a bit in awe of him, Heike thought, as he waved away the cakes she offered him.

"As I'm sure you'll understand, my dear," began Lotte nervously, "we can only give you an outline of what we're planning."

"No, no. I do understand," Heike said quickly. "But how many people are involved in this?"

"We're a large group, and we're all working on different projects," replied Lotte rather vaguely, "but *our* project is the one that is the most vital because…" she paused for a moment, choosing her words carefully, "because it may involve approaching Mikhail Gorbachev himself."

"You mean we're going to Russia!" exclaimed Heike, horrified. "That would be impossible."

"No, no," broke in Dietrich impatiently. "Gorbachev is coming here to East Berlin to meet with Mielke and Honecker. There are going to be big celebrations on the 7th of October, because the GDR will be celebrating forty years of existence, and that's when we'll possibly have a chance of getting close to him."

"But to do what?" asked Heike, puzzled by his explanation. "And why me, and how would we get to Berlin?"

Lotte could see that Heike was getting rather panicky and shot a warning glance at her son.

"The journey is the least of our problems," she said soothingly. "The main difficulty is getting you close enough to Gorbachev and giving you the opportunity to present our petition. Hundreds of us have signed it, and as you're a Russian speaker, which we aren't, that might be helpful."

Dietrich interrupted her again, "We're going to design some banners asking Russia to continue supporting East Germany and we hope these will catch Gorbachev's eye as he drives past."

Heike sat there silently for several minutes, mulling over what the pair of them had just said. Though the difficulties seemed insurmountable, the idea certainly sounded innocuous enough. However, there was something about this crazy plan and her involvement in it which didn't ring true as if some part of it was being hidden from her. Mother and son watched her as she deliberated the pros and cons of what she had been asked to do and what might lie behind all of this. Recent events since her arrival in Jena had made her very suspicious indeed, even of someone like Lotte who appeared so kind and friendly. Lotte glanced at

Dietrich questioningly, and he leant forward towards Heike, his manner becoming more conciliatory.

"You'd be doing a service for your country, you know," he said encouragingly, "and if you succeed, you might save East Germany from being wiped off the map. Isn't it worth the effort?"

"Are you asking me to do all this alone?" asked Heike, alarmed at the prospect.

"No, no, of course not, Heike," answered Lotte reassuringly. "We'd be there with you as moral support displaying the banners—Dietrich and me and probably Dietrich's wife Kristina, and maybe some others in our unit."

Heike fell silent again, thinking about what they were suggesting. She still had the impression that they were holding something back. "So, we'd travel to Berlin together then," she said slowly.

"No," replied Dietrich. "We'd all travel separately, and we'd send you your travel instructions just before we go in about two weeks' time."

Heike glanced at the date on her watch. Today was the 23rd. This was all so sudden and unexpected and didn't give her long to decide. She looked at Lotte again and wondered if she should, could trust her, or if she even wanted to be a part of this. There were so many aspects of life here that were unsatisfactory. Big changes needed to be made. Yet, it could be that a breathing space was needed, as Lotte had said, to achieve these freedoms.

What should I do? She thought to herself. For reasons that she couldn't explain, she sensed that something much more sinister lay behind the project. Some of the things they were saying somehow just did not ring true. Perhaps, she should play along with them a little and try and find out more. If she showed that she didn't trust them now, they'd just clam up on her and she'd never find out the truth. Her curiosity was aroused. She glanced at Lotte, who was studying her anxiously as if her life depended on what Heike's decision might be.

"Please help us, Heike," she said pleadingly. "It might be our last chance. The trouble with all these old men we've got at the top is that they'd never introduce any reforms, so this is why we've got all this dissent. If Gorby goes soft on us as he's planning to do, there'll be civil war, and then, the almost certain collapse of our country. We've got to buy some more time to give us the chance of campaigning to get a change of leadership—then we might have a chance of survival." She looked at Heike to see what impression her words had had.

"So, if the opportunity arises, I'd simply hand over your petition, asking Gorbachev to support us for a bit longer," said Heike slowly, "and then just say something to him if I get the chance—nothing more."

"Exactly," said Lotte, relieved. "Nothing more, and then we'd all come back to Jena together."

Heike deliberated with herself. It all seemed too pat, too well-rehearsed. *Perhaps, I should say I'll think about it*, she thought, *and then I'll see if I can get more out of Lotte nearer the time.* She pretended to be mulling over her decision for a few more moments before finally saying that she would like to help them, but wanted a few days to think it over.

Dietrich shook her warmly by the hand and Lotte embraced her. "Let me know as soon as you decide, my dear, and come round any time you want to. If, as we hope, you say yes, then we'll send you all the instructions for the journey and anything else you need to know."

Heike promised that she'd be in touch in the next few days. It was only as she made her way home that she wondered how Lotte had known that she spoke Russian.

Chapter 16

The Dean was very understanding when Maggie told her that she wanted to interrupt her studies for a couple of terms for personal reasons and continue her degree on her return. Maggie was grateful for her lack of questioning and her placid acceptance of Maggie's rather halting explanation. She had had to steal herself for this interview and was dreading that rather more in-depth reasons would be required by Dr Trenchard. However, the Dean merely referred to Maggie's grades for the year and reassured her that they were perfectly satisfactory. It was also with great relief that Maggie received the news that a change of tutor was a high probability as Professor Stowkovsky was likely to be taking his deferred sabbatical in the near future. Maggie had no difficulty in assuring the Dean that this would be no problem.

"Are you really sure you're happy with that, Maggie? Most students like to keep the same tutor for the time they're here."

"No, that's absolutely fine, Dr Trenchard," Maggie assured her hastily.

She fancied that the Dean looked at her rather keenly over her horn-rimmed spectacles and wondered if she'd been too pointed with her swift response. However, Dr Trenchard then rose to her feet, signalling that the interview was at an end and dismissed Maggie by saying kindly that she would look forward to seeing her the following year and to keep in touch by letter or e-mail if necessary.

Maggie made her way back to college to collect her things, keeping a sharp lookout for the tall figure of Nicholas Stowkovsky. The very last thing she wanted to do was to bump into him after their last encounter. For two or three days afterwards, Maggie had gone around in a daze, unwilling to confide even to Angie the events of that awful meeting. Anyway, her friend had her own problems with a divorce pending. She could not obliterate the image of Nicholas's dark, stormy face the moment before he had kissed her so angrily. Her emotions were in such a state of confusion that she didn't know how she felt about him.

Although she had been aware of a certain frisson between them for some time, in reality, his behaviour had been so mercurial that this sudden passionate embrace had been totally unexpected. She was angry and upset in equal measure and too numb to really decide what her own true feelings towards him were. All she knew for certain was that she must get away from Oxford for the time being, in case she turned a corner and suddenly came face to face with him.

Through the internal mail, he had sent the books she had left behind in his study in her rush to get away. The parcel was accompanied by a curt note in which he apologised briefly and asked if she would meet him in a place of her own choosing as he wished to speak to her to offer an explanation in person for his behaviour. Maggie had replied with a stiff message saying that she accepted his apology, but as far as she was concerned, the matter was at an end. She had since then lived in constant fear of him suddenly appearing in the library or the Ashdown. It was after three days spent creeping furtively around, trying to avoid everyone she knew, that Maggie decided to have a break in her studies. She recognised she just had to escape from Oxford for a few months and put some distance between the two of them while she rationalised what had happened.

During several sleepless nights, she puzzled over what her best plan of action might be. A plan was formulating in her mind to go to Jena, not only to do some research around the new ideas she'd been considering for her dissertation, but also to see if she could track down what had happened to Heike Stowkovsky. She wasn't really sure why she wanted to do this, partly curiosity, perhaps, but also because she dimly recognised that the torment for Nicholas was not knowing what had really happened to his wife. Inexplicably, it had become important for her to try and shed some light on Heike's disappearance.

It might at least bring him some peace of mind, she thought, trying to justify her decision to herself.

She avoided delving too deeply into her reasons for all of this but felt happier at having come to a decision. She wrote brief notes to her principal and to Angie, claiming a family bereavement for her sudden departure. There only remained a couple of tasks—one was to arrange for the storage of her caravan on the farm and the other, rather more sensitive one, was to pay a visit to Sue. If she was going to have any success in tracking down Heike, she needed more information about where she had been staying and what she had been doing in Jena. She couldn't think who else she could ask. She certainly couldn't approach Nicholas Stowkovsky.

Sue met her at the cottage door, obviously dying with curiosity about Maggie's unexpected visit and rather guarded phone call. Seeing Maggie's white, strained face, she immediately led her into the quiet sitting room and told her to sit down while she made some coffee. She sounded so sympathetic and so kind that poor Maggie distinguished herself by bursting into floods of tears. Sue, really worried now, sat down beside her and putting her arm round her, asked what the matter was. Maggie sobbed even harder on Sue's shoulder, but after a few minutes, blew her nose really hard and blurted out all that had happened between herself and Nicholas.

Sue was silent for several minutes before saying, "What a fool the man is! He needs a good talking to—he's in love with you, you know," she added unexpectedly.

Maggie, red-eyed, looked unconvinced as she sniffed into her handkerchief and said gruffly that she never wanted to see Nicholas Stowkovsky again. She'd had enough of him. Sue, smiling a little at that, tactfully left her for a few minutes while she went to make some coffee. By the time she returned, Maggie was more composed and began apologising in a rather shamefaced way for burdening Sue with all her troubles.

"Nonsense," said Sue briskly as she gave Maggie a large mug of milky coffee. "That's what friends are for, and I'm truly sorry that Nicholas can't sort his emotions out and come to his senses—you'd be so good together."

"Well, I'm not interested in him, and anyhow, I'm going away," retorted Maggie, red-faced at that comment. "So, it'll give him time to see to his own affairs without a troublesome, mature student to bother with. I only seem to make him angry all the time."

Seeing Sue's shocked and surprised face, Maggie explained her plans and then asked for information regarding Heike. Sue's eyes narrowed as she listened to Maggie's request.

"Why do you want to go to all this trouble to find out what happened to Heike? You didn't even know her."

Maggie looked her straight in the eye and said, without stopping to think, "Because I believe it's destroying Nicholas, this not knowing."

Sue looked at her keenly. "And why are you so concerned about that, Maggie? You've just said you're not interested in him. I believe you're in love with him and don't want to admit it."

Maggie half-opened her mouth to deny this and then thought better of it as she looked at Sue's sharp gaze. "I don't know how I feel," she answered frankly, "but I think if I go away, it will give us both space, and if I do unearth something, it might bring him peace of mind and a chance to move on in his life. I have the impression from different things you've told me that he believes Heike got involved in some political intrigue and that he's finding this difficult to live with. Comments he made here when we were all together made me feel he can never be happy until he knows one way or the other."

Sue nodded slowly in agreement and, after a few minutes' thought, told Maggie at length all she knew about Heike and what she had been doing in East Germany. "Nicholas lost contact with her about the end of September 1989," she continued, "and with everything in such a turmoil in East Germany at that time, it was very difficult to get any sense out of anybody, but," she concluded, "it's nearly three years since she disappeared. I should've thought that all traces of her would have vanished by now. I'm not sure that you'll have any more success than he did. He made several visits there and got nowhere."

Despite this rather pessimistic assessment, everything that Sue had told her made Maggie all the more determined to do some detective work of her own. Sue was obviously concerned about her proposed trip and tried to dissuade her, but seeing she was not to be deflected, made her promise to be careful and to keep in contact.

As she waved goodbye, she was wondering if she'd done the right thing giving Maggie all that information regarding Heike. Nicholas left her in no doubt when he told her in no uncertain terms what he thought of her stupidity. He had come round to find out if Sue knew anything of Maggie's whereabouts or if by chance Maggie had called in. He was beside himself with feelings of guilt at the way he'd treated Maggie and disturbed that he had not been able to meet her as he'd wanted to. After reading her stiff note, he had spent two or three days wandering miserably around Oxford, hoping for sight of her, but to no avail.

"She's gone where?" he exclaimed angrily when Sue told him rather shamefacedly what Maggie's plans were and that she'd helped her by giving her all the information she had asked for. She had never seen Nicholas so worried and angry, and when she tried to reassure him by saying that Maggie was too sensible to get into any trouble, he silenced her with a withering look and asked her if she knew when Maggie was leaving for Germany.

Sue shook her head. "I'm sorry, Nicholas but I really don't know—I think she's going to her flat in London first, but I don't have the address."

"Was she very unhappy?" he broke in abruptly. Sue was silent for a moment. "I suppose that's a 'yes'," he said grimly.

"I've seen her happier," replied Sue, remembering Maggie's floods of tears. "What do you expect after the way you treated her? She's worried about you, though Lord knows why, which is one reason she's going to Jena."

"Little fool," retorted Nicholas. "I can sort out my own problems."

Sue looked at him sceptically. "Well, you're not making a very good job of it, are you?" She was about to say more but didn't want to add to his unhappiness.

After saying a rather frosty goodbye to her, Nicholas made his way back to Oxford, wondering whether Maggie might have spoken to Jutta by any chance—could that wretched woman have encouraged Maggie to set off on this madcap trip? He had not had much contact with Jutta over the last few months and had tended to avoid events where he thought they might meet, so he didn't really want to seek her out. He sat in his study for some time, pondering as to what he should do. He urgently needed to discover what Maggie's exact plans were but was at a loss to know whom to ask. If she hadn't confided in Sue, who else might she have spoken to?

He was rather reluctant to ask her student friends and start any gossip circulating. Then it occurred to him that if she had decided to have a break in her studies, then she must have discussed the possibility of this with Dr Trenchard, so perhaps, the best thing would be to have a word with her. However, he drew a blank there. The Dean raised an eyebrow when he asked for information, obviously thinking that Maggie would have gone to her supervisor first as a matter of courtesy. But she could shed no further light on Maggie's movements.

"She just told me she wanted a break for a while," was all the information he got from her.

She found the matter curious enough to mention to a close friend and colleague over coffee in the Senior Common Room later that evening. Jutta, hearing Nicholas's name, pricked up her ears and stood as close as she dared—ostensibly helping herself to more coffee. Her curiosity was aroused by the Dean's puzzlement at the detailed nature of Nicholas's questions and his obvious interest in this particular student.

"Surely, he couldn't be emotionally involved with her, could he?" Jutta heard Dr Trenchard say, and then, seeing Jutta standing nearby, lowered her voice so that Jutta was unable to hear anymore. Her lips tightened to a thin line; it had been several weeks since she had had any contact with Nicholas, and even that had been very brief and formal. Though she had been striving to deny it to herself for some time, it had finally dawned on her now that Nicholas was avoiding her at all costs. Why should he spurn her so, when they had once been so close? Now that Heike was not on the scene, she had hoped he might drift back to her and had tried her best to entice him, but to no avail.

It had become an obsession with her to make some impact on him, but he appeared oblivious to her presence. She wished she could punish and hurt him for the way he had behaved towards her. Perhaps, she would find out a little more about this Maggie, and why Nicholas was so concerned about her, and whether she had yet another rival.

"I know. I'll go and have a word with Edith," she said to herself. "She's got all the student files. I'm sure I can dig something out."

She had a friend in the Graduate Office, and she decided that she would go in there tomorrow morning and see what she could find out. Edith, though surprised about her queries, was able to give her quite a lot of information about the nature of Maggie's work and the progress she had made. As Jutta studied Maggie's file, she noted that rather than living in college, she had been staying on a farm in Eaton. She made a mental note of the address before handing the papers back to Edith with profuse thanks.

"Don't let anyone know I've shown this to you, will you, Jutta?" Edith said nervously. "I could get into trouble. This is all confidential material, as you know." Jutta promised her as she hurried away.

A quick visit to the farmhouse pretending to be one of Maggie's tutors elicited Maggie's London address, and she was just about to leave when Richard unexpectedly told her that Maggie had also left a forwarding address in Germany. He rummaged around in the untidy piles of paper on his office desk, and when he finally produced the scrap of paper on which he had scribbled the information, Jutta glanced at it and could hardly believe what she was seeing. She stopped breathing momentarily as the words 'Friedrich Schiller Universitat, Jena' seemed to leap out of the page at her.

She missed Nicholas by only half an hour. Having had no luck with discreet enquiries at Maggie's College, he arrived at the farm as a last resort.

"You're the second person to be asking after Maggie Stewart today," Richard informed him cheerfully, as he gave Nicholas the same information he had given

Jutta. "A tall, thin woman was here about half an hour ago—brown hair, wrong side of fifty—said she was one of Maggie's tutors."

"Jutta," muttered Nicholas through gritted teeth. "Now what the hell's she playing at?"

He would have been even more concerned if he had overheard her phone calls to Germany and seen the spiteful, satisfied look on her face as she put the receiver down.

Chapter 17

"Whatever am I going to do?" mused Heike aloud. She had reached a crisis point; that much she knew. She checked the date on her watch. Time was running out; only a week to go before Gorbachev arrived in East Berlin. She stared out of the window thoughtfully. The watchers were there as usual—no change there, then. Their unvarying pattern had, in a strange way, become a comfort.

What on Earth am I doing here, mixed up in a harebrained scheme like this? She thought to herself. *I must be crazy, getting involved in something that perhaps is going to lead me into further danger.* She had a helpless sense of being drawn into a deep pit where she was totally out of her depth. Events somehow had spiralled out of control, and yet, at first, she'd believed that it was her moral duty to find out what was being planned or possibly help her own country in some way. Now, however, she was not so sure.

There was also this uneasy sense that something rather more sinister lurked behind the plan, another agenda that she had not been made party to and had still not been able to discover. She had paid another visit to Lotte, but Dietrich had also been there, and with his brooding presence, Lotte had been unwilling to divulge any more information. All she had been prepared to do was to put further pressure on Heike to let them know her decision as soon as possible. Heike had come away feeling even more stressed and confused.

"I must go and see Lotte again and see whether I can find her alone this time," she decided. "Perhaps, I could then press her a bit more about what's going on, and if I can't, I'll tell her that I've changed my mind and have decided to pull out."

She felt rather apprehensive about going back to see Lotte without first finding out if Dietrich was still in the house. She knew she'd have much more chance of gradually persuading the old lady to tell her more about their plans without her son's glowering presence. The only problem was that she didn't know how to be sure of finding Lotte on her own without visiting the house again and taking a chance. Any alternatives were out of the question—her phone was tapped, she was sure, and a letter posted asking to speak to her alone wouldn't achieve anything and could simply arouse suspicion. Anyway, the postal system was very unreliable, and time was running out.

"I suppose I could just turn up," she mused, "and if Dietrich is still there, I'd just have to make some excuse and leave. Tell them I'll come back another time."

That seemed a bit risky, though, as they might start questioning her about her resolve to stay part of the group, and her unease might show through. Her thoughts whirled round and round in her mind as she weighed up the pros and cons. Her strong curiosity about the whole setup finally overcame any misgivings she had about her foolhardiness, and she decided in the end to write a brief note to Lotte to simply ask if she could pop round and have some tea with her on her own the next day. This seemed innocuous enough, and she could deliver it this afternoon. She felt calmer at having come to a decision.

It was lunchtime when she set off and the streets were quiet, just the sound of her own quick footsteps echoing through the tiny, cobbled alleyways. At one point, however, she was convinced that she had heard footsteps other than her own. She turned quickly, but could see no one. Then, a few minutes later, the sound again. Heike checked over her shoulder. A shadow slipped into a doorway; yes, she was being followed, she was certain. Her mouth dry, she quickened her steps, her heart pounding, but the other person kept pace with her. Heike was so shaken that by the time she reached Lotte's house, she inadvertently knocked on the door. She cursed herself for her stupidity, but before she could slip the letter into the letterbox and make her escape, Lotte flung open the door as if she'd been expecting her.

"Good to see you, little Heike," she murmured, but her smile of welcome was tight and forced and she appeared nervous and on edge as she grasped Heike's arm and pulled her inside.

"No, really, I can't stay," protested Heike, thrusting her letter into Lotte's hand, but in vain—the elderly woman was insistently ushering her into the sitting room and remained between her and the door. Lotte opened Heike's letter, her face becoming graver by the minute.

"Why did you want to see me alone, my dear? I hope you weren't thinking of letting us down," she said finally, her voice wavering a little. "Perhaps you'd better wait here a moment."

Heike tried to explain further, but Lotte was gone. To her horror, Heike heard the key turn in the lock. She was trapped, but why? Her heart thumping, Heike tiptoed across the room and put her ear to the keyhole. She could clearly hear people speaking—a man's voice she did not recognise raised in anger.

"You stupid, old woman, you said she was one of us, could be trusted."

Heike strained to catch Lotte's reply, but instead heard her cry out in pain, then the man's voice again, mocking this time. It was not Dietrich, she was sure.

"You were told, you were told, how do you know this source of yours was reliable?" Once again, she could not make out Lotte's reply.

Heavy footsteps sounded in the hallway, and Heike sprang away from the doorway just in time as it was thrown open with some force, and a tall, thin, sallow-skinned man strode in. His prickly blonde hair was cropped military short, and his pale blue eyes fixed Heike with an expressionless gaze. The way he was looking at her with a slightly mocking smile convinced Heike that he had been today's unknown stalker.

"Why were you following me?" she challenged him, her voice trembled despite her best efforts.

His contemptuous smile deepened. "Got to keep an eye on any possible waverers."

Heike took a deep breath. Moral duty or not, she had to escape from this situation. She gripped the table in front of her. "I've decided I don't want to be a part of the group anymore. I'm sorry."

"I'm sorry, too," he replied silkily. "The choice isn't yours to make."

"You can't force me," countered Heike, her voice still sounding quavery to her ears.

"Oh, can't I?" he smirked, his heavy-lidded eyes cold, uncaring. "Just watch me."

Heike shivered involuntarily, then tried to sound braver than she felt. "Well, I'm going now, and whatever you say, I shan't change my mind." She made a move towards the doorway, but he stood unmoving, blocking her way.

At that moment, she realised that Lotte had come in from an adjoining room. Her eyes were red as if she had been crying, and there was a livid bruise on one side of her face.

"Let her go, Axel," she pleaded. "She'll be discreet, I'm sure. And she doesn't know very much, anyway."

He wheeled round, his arm raised, his face contorted with fury. "I told you to stay out of this. You're useless, and you've caused enough harm already, bringing this troublemaker in—she certainly knows too much now to let her wander off like some loose cannon."

Lotte cringed and seemed to shrivel, her eyes wide and frightened like a cornered rabbit. Axel turned back towards Heike—his eyes with their pale lashes held a hidden menace.

An inner chill gripped her. *He'd kill me without a second's thought*, she felt certain. He pulled an envelope out of his pocket and handed it to her, and she took it with trembling fingers.

"Open it."

Heike was shocked and surprised. Inside was a photo of her and Nicholas standing outside the Bodleian. His arm was around her shoulders, and he was laughing straight into the camera. With a catch in her throat, Heike realised it had been taken by Sue when the four of them were celebrating Nicholas's birthday last year.

Axel was studying her reaction. "Happy memories, eh?" he sneered. "Now, see here; if you don't cooperate fully with us, your beloved husband will die a lingering death."

As Heike looked at the photo, tears filled her eyes. The panic that was just beneath the surface broke through, paralysing her so that she could hardly breathe.

"Please, no, you couldn't. You wouldn't," she whispered.

"We certainly could and would; make no mistake about it. We have many agents operating in Oxford—it needs only a word from me, and he'd die a long, lingering death."

Axel noted her white face with satisfaction. "Remember what I've said—fully cooperate. We'll be keeping an eye on you all the time. We have watchers everywhere, so don't even think of leaving or running to the authorities for help. You'll get your instructions in a day or so." He put his face right up to hers, grasping her shoulder so that she couldn't back away. His powerful fingers seemed to bite into her flesh. "Follow them to the letter." He released her and stood aside. "You're free to go." He pushed her roughly towards the door.

As Heike, trembling uncontrollably, stumbled and half fell into the narrow street, she could still hear Axel's final words ringing in her ears. "If you love your husband, you make sure you behave."

Chapter 18

Maggie, blissfully unaware of all the interest in her movements, closed up her London flat and set off for Jena a week after leaving Oxford. She was glad to be busy, organising her trip to Germany and thankful to have something to occupy her mind. Her sister had not been convinced when Maggie, rather haltingly, had made some lame excuse as to why she was leaving Oxford for a few months.

"What do you mean, you feel a bit stressed? What are you hiding, Maggie?"

"Nothing. I just want a break for a while." Maggie felt cornered.

In the end, she was forced to give in to her sister's persistent questioning and confided to Jenny the real reason for her sudden departure. Her sister had been incredulous.

"You never hinted that he felt like that about you."

"I don't know what he feels. It was nothing concrete you could put into words, just an atmosphere till that day." Maggie had been defensive. "Don't make so much of it, Jenny."

"Why on Earth didn't you meet him as he wanted? You might've felt better about everything," insisted Jenny.

Maggie looked at her younger sister, so different from herself, a warm-hearted, bubbly, outgoing personality. For Jenny, things were more cut and dried. She would leap into action impulsively, without any thought of the consequences or weighing up the pros and cons and how she might be affected in her rush to put things right.

"You weren't there. You can't even imagine how I felt—the shock of it." Maggie's voice wavered a little, and Jenny, tactful for once, didn't pursue the point.

After that meeting with her sister, the whole devastating episode had been brought back into her mind from the deepest recesses where she'd been trying to hide it. Maggie decided she must now focus on all the planning that had to be done and try to take control of her life again. She'd decided it might be better if she put up at a hotel to start with while she sorted out what she wanted to do with herself. A quick trawl on the internet picked up the Holiday Inn just outside the city centre which sounded perfect. On her arrival there, she felt she'd made a good choice.

I'll just have a few days' relaxation, she thought as she settled in, *and then I'll get in contact with the university.*

She knew she'd have to search around for a room or a flat to rent somewhere near the university, which would be a much cheaper option long-term, and she'd then have a base to work from. The university authorities in Jena were very helpful when Maggie finally approached them and explained her background and the work she was interested in doing. Having organised her studies, she waited a few weeks before embarking on any detective work and divided her time pleasantly between the university and exploring the town. Although Jena was now part of a united Germany, in that summer of 1992, there were still many signs of the old East Germany and little evidence of the prosperity permeating through from the West. People remained wary of strangers, and Maggie planned to keep a low profile until she was accepted. This turned out to be longer than she had expected, and it was not until she'd been in Jena for about four weeks that she started making any real contacts.

The lovely old university was more or less as she'd imagined it with its beautiful fourteenth architecture and peaceful courtyards. She spent several days exploring it and its surroundings with its constant reminders of Goethe and Schiller. She tried to put Nicholas out of her mind, but thoughts of Oxford kept drifting uninvited into her waking moments.

She realised on reflection that she should have asked for a change of supervisor in the Michaelmas term, but the ethos of Oxford generated a respect and awe for academic achievement that made a professor seem a venerable being that you did not question. She wondered idly what a younger student would've done. Perhaps, her generation had more respect for a figure like Professor Stowkovsky and weren't prepared to question their authority in the same way. She ended up as always with no answers, just a feeling of regret and dissatisfaction. Despite these sad thoughts, she enjoyed all her exploration, travelling by tram and becoming familiar with all the stops en route from the hotel and smiling at some of the names intoned through the intercom as the tram rattled along.

'Paradies Bahnhof' was one that particularly amused her, as that particular station certainly bore no resemblance to any paradise she knew but looked rather tatty and in need of some restoration! As she wandered around and finally began doing some study in the attractive old library, she became more of a familiar figure to those working and studying there and often joined other students as they toiled up the hill to the Mensa or canteen for lunch.

It was during one of these visits that she unexpectedly made her most important contact to date. As she moved towards a table with her tray one lunchtime, she stumbled over a briefcase left on the floor and half fell against a table where a dark-haired woman was drinking some coffee. As it spilt all over the table, Maggie, greatly embarrassed, apologised profusely and insisted on buying her another cup of coffee. On her return, she was invited to sit down and join her new acquaintance who introduced herself as Marta Neubert.

"I'm Maggie Stewart," Maggie volunteered, looking at Marta with interest. She was a tall, striking woman, about Maggie's age, with dark, slanting eyes giving her rather an oriental appearance, her thick, dark hair fashionably cut.

"Where are you from, Maggie?" she asked, sipping her coffee. When Maggie told her and explained that she was doing some research on East German literature and in particular Christa Wolf, she thought Marta looked at her for a moment as if she was about to say something, but then thinking better of it, said, "Your German's very good, Maggie. Have you studied in Germany before?"

Maggie blushed as she always did on receiving a compliment. "I just did one or two summer schools when I was younger." She looked at the other woman and thought she looked vaguely familiar. "Why are you here, Marta?" she asked. "Are you a student too?"

Marta laughed. "I'm one of the tutors," she replied. "My specialism is Russian literature." When Maggie started to say sorry, she brushed her apologies aside. "It's such a large university, it'll take some time before you get to know everyone, and there've been quite a lot of changes in the last couple of years since the collapse of the GDR."

She was a good listener, and Maggie soon found herself talking about her Russian studies at Oxford.

Marta looked at her with a new interest. "You've obviously done a lot of in-depth research in this, haven't you? You're really on top of it all. But what puzzles me is why you broke off your studies to come here. I should think Oxford has much better facilities than we have here."

She would've questioned her more, but when Maggie falteringly and unconvincingly tried to explain about a change of ideas, she became aware that this was rather a sore topic, and tactfully suggested that they walked back to the university together. After that first meeting, they started having lunch regularly and, finding they had a lot in common, began taking trips out together to places like Weimar and Leipzig.

Marta was an excellent guide and filled in the gaps in Maggie's knowledge about the cultural life of this part of former East Germany. As they got to know each other better, she even started talking in a more personal way about what life had been like under the DDR regime. It was obviously a painful subject, so Maggie was careful not to press her too hard, although she was beginning to hope that Marta might be able to provide some clues as to what could have happened to Heike.

One day, when they were walking back to the university after lunch, Maggie asked Marta casually whether there had been many Stasi informants on the academic staff.

"About half of us informed on the other half," Marta informed her dryly, "and many of them left when the Stasi files were opened at the end of 1990. Once it was made possible for people to check whether they'd been spied on, many couldn't face the accusing eyes and pointing fingers."

Maggie looked at her, wide-eyed. "Us? You mean you were a Stasi informer?" Marta glanced at her briefly, and Maggie thought her eyes had a haunted look. "I was given no choice," she said abruptly and then refused to be drawn further.

Maggie didn't see her for several days and felt that she'd perhaps overstepped the mark and that Marta was now avoiding her. She finally wrote Marta a brief note, saying that she hoped she hadn't offended her in any way and that she wanted to meet as she had something very important she wanted to ask her. Maggie realised that she was running the risk of alienating Marta, but she sensed that this new friend was her best chance of shedding light on Heike's disappearance and she had to take a chance.

When she found a hastily scribbled note waiting for her next morning, suggesting meeting at a nearby pub that evening, she breathed a sigh of relief. Marta arrived, as elegant as ever, carrying a small leather book which she placed on the table between them. When the waiter had brought them their order of sandwiches and a bottle of wine, there was a moment's silence, and then Marta said unexpectedly, "You want to know about Heike Stowkovsky, don't you? That's why you're really here."

Maggie was struck dumb for a moment, but there seemed no point in subterfuge "H… How did you know?" she stuttered.

Marta smiled grimly. "You were a bit transparent with all those questions. It didn't take much working out—she was from Oxford, too, doing the same study on Christa as you and similar in age. I suppose you were friends."

When Maggie, who was taken aback at the speed and turn of events, explained rather awkwardly that she'd never known Heike, only her husband, Marta looked at her rather disbelievingly. "Did he send you to look for her?" she asked, looking at Maggie sharply. "He came out here himself, you know, asking questions, just after…" She broke off for a moment. "Just after her disappearance." She poured out a glass of wine for them both before she continued.

Maggie, rather red-faced, explained that Nicholas didn't even know that she was in Jena and that it had been her own idea because she was concerned about his mental state. Marta raised an eyebrow but made no comment. She seemed absorbed in her own thoughts and a little unsure as to where to begin. She finally gave Maggie a potted history of Heike's arrival and early days in Jena, most of which Maggie knew from what Sue had told her.

"Initially," Marta continued, "her visit seemed innocuous enough, but when she started visiting known dissidents, I was assigned to set up surveillance on her. The normal things—observation, phone-taps, post checked," she said it almost casually.

"Did you tell her husband this when he came over?" asked Maggie, shocked at all of this.

"No, of course I didn't," snapped Marta. "He came over at a particularly sensitive time, and I certainly wasn't going to blow my cover."

Maggie, pondering on what Marta had said, visualised Nicholas so anxious and afraid about Heike and felt a sudden burst of anger. "How could you do this, Marta? Aren't you ashamed of yourself?"

"How dare you pass judgement on me!" said Marta angrily, two high spots of colour on her normally pale face. "You've no idea what life was like here and what pressures were brought to bear on us, and whether you would have acted any differently if you'd been in my place. It's very easy to take the moral high ground when you look back on these events from a distance." Maggie fell silent, and Marta looked at her for a moment before continuing, "I had no choice," she said bluntly. "It was that or no job. You didn't say no to the Stasi—if you got on the wrong side of them, it was then very difficult to find work again. You might get interviews where you were told you were just the person they were looking for and then receive a letter saying that they'd found someone else more suitable—you were effectively blacklisted. I couldn't afford that. I had my son Erich to support."

Maggie glanced at her ringless fingers. "I didn't know you were married," she said slowly.

"My husband went over the Wall in the seventies," replied Marta in a matter-of-fact way. "A group of them went from his factory on a business trip. The others came back, but he opted to stay behind."

"Didn't you want to join him?" asked Maggie.

"That's a long story, but basically, no. I felt a certain loyalty to the GDR and had a secure job—the future was uncertain for those who went over to the West. Erich was at a good school and was happy there."

Maggie felt an unexpected surge of sympathy for her in that predicament and with her torn loyalties. "Is your son still at home with you?"

"No," said Marta with bitterness in her voice. "As soon as he was old enough, he joined his father—you see, he found out I was working for the Stasi."

Maggie looked at her curiously. "And you didn't want to join them both?"

Marta shrugged her shoulders. "No point. My husband had found a girlfriend by then."

Maggie now understood the haunted look in her brown eyes. "Did you have to do…" she paused, uncertain how to continue.

"Things that threatened people's lives?" broke in Marta with a wry grimace. "The answer to that is that I don't really know what they did with my information. I'm not making any excuses for what I did. We all do things we regret in our lives. Everyone is flawed in some way. We are all of us, carrying around some burden or another which affects how we behave and the decisions we make—but you have to put yourself in my position at the time." She paused before pushing the slim, leather notebook across the table to Maggie. "However, with Heike, it was different. I really did know, because when I read this, I realised that I may have caused her death."

Chapter 19

The crowds were much larger than Heike had anticipated, standing at least twenty feet deep at the most advantageous spot to get a good view of the podium. There were red flags as far as the eye could see, and the crowds were already beginning their chant of 'Gorby, Gorby'. Despite all the protests from those around, by dint of pushing and shoving, Heike was engineered to the front by Dietrich and Kristina. Fortunately, the crowd was largely good-humoured, and Kristina explained that her friend was a visitor eager to see democracy at work. The throng grew even denser as the time for President Gorbachev to arrive drew nearer. As Heike stood there, waiting with the others, a kaleidoscope of thoughts swirling around in her mind after that momentous conversation with Axel on the train to Berlin. She was aware of his watchful, brooding presence close behind her in that crowd of people, lowering her spirits even further. He had so enjoyed dropping that bombshell and observing her horrified reaction. It seemed like a bad omen. She closed her eyes momentarily, trying to blot out the events earlier that day, with little success.

The morning had started badly. In the early hours, she had woken up with a sick feeling of dread and a premonition that a terrible event was about to take place. She had had only fitful sleep; in fact, she hadn't really slept well since that nightmarish confrontation with Axel at Lotte's. The night following her last visit there, she had been unable to sleep at all, but had lain awake, tossing and turning until the morning light streamed in through her bedroom window. Every time she closed her eyes, she saw Axel's hard, implacable face as he threatened her and Nicholas.

He had been deadly serious; she knew that for sure. There were dreadful poisons that could be used that left little trace in the human body. She was conscious of this fact only too well. She had read enough about Nazi brutality to be fully aware of their existence and the slow, agonising death that resulted in their use. Now, the fateful day of action had arrived, and her mouth was dry from nerves. She was feeling like a trapped animal unable to make its escape. She had

had no further contact with any of the group but wondered if they were watching her as Axel had threatened.

She had tried to phone Lotte the night before, more for reassurance than anything else, but yet again, the line was not functioning, and she now felt a moment of blind panic as if caught up in a spider's web with no way out. She was of half a mind to walk away from this whole mad escapade despite Axel's threats and go straight back to England and warn Nicholas. Surely, together they could work something out, go into hiding, perhaps, up in Scotland with Alex, Nicholas's sister, where they would be safe. But as she clutched at the comfort of this idea, she remembered again with an inner chill the dire warnings she had received. No, she had to see this through, whatever the consequences. She was now inextricably involved.

Her instructions had arrived as promised—a mysterious white envelope appearing yet again under her door, with neither sight nor sound of the person delivering it. She was told to catch the early-morning train via Leipzig to East Berlin on 7th October and to expect further contact to be made at some stage on her train journey. The money for the fare was enclosed. Her backpack lay on the floor, ready and waiting for her departure, and she had a strange feeling of comfort at the familiar sight of it and a sense of liberation. Once today was over, she could put a distance between herself and Lotte's associates, she told herself.

She'd resolved to leave Jena for a while and, rather than go back to Oxford straightaway, had formulated a plan to explore the area around Meckleburg, not only to further her research but also to delve into her own family history and perhaps lay a few ghosts. Depending on how she got on, she might then even go back to Jena, she thought. Despite all the pressure that had been put on her, Heike had made up her mind not to be cowed, even though this constant niggling fear was beginning to take its toll. She was reluctant to return home directly before her three months were up in spite of all that had happened, and this seemed to her an attractive and relatively safe option. She reasoned to herself that after today, interest in her might dwindle.

If I leave Jena for a while, she thought, *I might avoid further risk of possible reprisals from all these people like Axel and those Russians who've been threatening me.*

She packed only the essentials she would need for a few weeks away, and as she'd paid the full three months' rental, she reckoned she could safely leave the rest of her possessions to be collected upon her return. She had felt a sense of relief at having come to this decision. She needed to make use of this enforced trip to Berlin. Despite the unpleasant circumstances surrounding it, it was perhaps offering her the opportunity of taking a more proactive grip on her life. As the waves of panic threatened to overwhelm her in the grey light of dawn, she reviewed the plans she had made and decided to get up and put a few last minute provisions in her backpack. After some consideration, she decided to leave her journal behind, safely tucked away in its usual hiding place. It was just something else to carry. Once she got underway, she reckoned she'd feel a lot calmer.

It was not until she was just half an hour away from the environs of East Berlin that Axel made contact with her. Her heart sank as he suddenly appeared in front of her and sat down in the opposite seat. So, he was to be her travelling companion. For all she knew, he'd been observing her for the whole journey. His pale blue eyes fixed on her with a sardonic gaze, but today, he was a man of few words. After handing her a single sheet of paper which he explained was the speech she had to read if the chance arose, he lapsed into a silent scrutiny as if weighing her up in some way. Heike found his hard, unblinking gaze unnerving and decided to challenge him in an attempt to assert herself.

"Why did you choose to inveigle me into your enterprise? There must have been scores of others you could have bullied instead."

He fixed her with a cold glare, obviously irritated by her choice of language. "But not with a husband who is an Oxford professor and a father who was a Stasi agent in Oxford after the war. That's very useful for making sure you do as you're told. I'm sure you don't want that leaking out—it wouldn't do your husband's career any good at all. You've also come with very good credentials, Lotte assures me."

Barely heeding his final comments, Heike gazed at him open-mouthed. "My father, a spy? That's impossible. He wouldn't have done anything to help the East German authorities. He hated them."

"He may have done," Axel looked at her sardonically. "But how else was he to fund himself in England and buy a bookshop in Oxford, which is, by the way, an extremely good place for recruiting and observing?" He smiled his thin, cruel smile. "And then, he had your brother to think of."

Heike was for a moment completely dumb struck. "Freddie! That can't be true," she croaked finally, finding it difficult to get the words out. "Out of the question. He died defending Berlin."

"You know that for sure?" Axel picked at one of his teeth. "I don't suppose you ever saw his body. In fact, he was captured by the Russians and sent to a labour camp. The authorities promised your father that they would try to get your brother released if he cooperated with them."

Heike gazed at him in silence. "But Freddie never came home," she said finally, in a faltering voice.

Axel shrugged his shoulders. "Par for the course, my dear. Politicians will promise anything to get what they want, we all know that, and your father kept on hoping."

Heike subsided, sinking back into her seat, utterly defeated. When they drew into Ostbahnhof, her hands were trembling and clammy as she fumbled inside her handbag for her ticket. She pulled her backpack down from the luggage rack and followed Axel onto the platform. He raised an eyebrow rather sardonically on seeing what she was carrying but made no comment. The only emotion he permitted himself was an obvious impatience at the delay in the station concourse while Heike organised a left-luggage locker for her possessions. As he hurried her along the narrow streets, he turned around from time to time, as if checking whether they were being followed.

Heike was not only overcome by the information that she had just received but she was also growing more and more uneasy about her own safety and ventured to ask where Lotte was. Axel was clearly surprised at her question as he replied sharply that an old woman like that had no place in today's enterprise. Her heart sank at the thought of being alone for the rest of the day with this taciturn, disagreeable man who had so clearly enjoyed tormenting her. It was therefore with some relief that she saw Dietrich's familiar figure emerge from a small black Wartburg, followed by Kristina.

Axel quickened his pace and hurried on ahead, and the three of them engaged in a muffled conversation. When Dietrich pointed rather impatiently at his watch and Axel gesticulated towards her, Heike guessed they were late for the rendezvous, and she was being blamed for it. She felt rather uncomfortable as she joined them, though Dietrich and Kristina greeted her pleasantly enough.

And now, here she was, amongst the surging throng of people, her heart thumping with nerves with the three of them in a semi-circle behind her. Despite her trepidation at what she had become involved in and what the outcome might be, Heike felt that there was safety in numbers. Surely, nothing very terrible could happen to her among so many people. She couldn't help but be caught up by the light-heartedness of the crowd and the party-like atmosphere. She even found herself chanting 'Gorby, Gorby' along with the rest. The crowd's excitement intensified as there were signs of preparation on the podium. Finally, in the distance, Heike could see the Soviet motorcade approaching, the motorcycle outriders forcing the crowds back as they surged forward. Heike transferred her sheet of paper from one damp hand to the other. The contents were just as Lotte had said, but her mouth felt dry, and she wondered vaguely where the banners were that they were supposed to be holding. What were the silent trio behind her really planning? She felt too preoccupied to ask. She just longed for the day to be over. The shouts of the people grew louder when they saw Mikhail Gorbachev smiling and waving as he heard the shouts, 'Gorby, Gorby, help us, help us!' Heike, now really involved in the atmosphere, waved her speech in the air and chanted with those around her.

As Gorbachev's limousine drew level with her, he glanced out of the window at one of the motorcyclists who appeared to be speaking to him and pointing in Heike's direction. The Russian President raised his hand, obviously giving some instruction, and the car came to a halt. As if in a dream, she could see him coming towards her, smiling and extending his hand; the crowd stretched out their arms. 'Gorby, Gorby!' Heike smiling too, in surprise, half-turned to share her excitement with the other three, who stood strangely silent, tucked in close behind her. To her horror, she observed a small, silver pistol in Axel's hand. Using her body as a shield, he raised it, aiming it directly at the Soviet leader as he approached them, waiting for just the right moment.

"No!" cried Heike frantically, thrusting his arm upwards. The silencer muffled the sound of the shot, and she felt a white-hot searing pain as the bullet passed through her chest.

"You stupid little bitch," hissed Dietrich as she slumped into his arms, a red stain spreading across her clothing.

Axel, muttering under his breath, quickly wrapped his coat around her, and he and Dietrich supported her limp body through the crowds, while the seemingly solicitous Kristina explained to those around that their poor friend had fainted with the excitement. The crowds, uncaring and unheeding, surged forward again and Gorbachev, ignorant of what had happened and of his narrow escape, and moved along the lines of eager faces, pressing people's hands.

Axel and Dietrich roughly manhandled Heike through the empty back streets, her feet dragging along the pavement as they hurried along. When they arrived at the car, they thrust her limp body unceremoniously onto the back seat and covered her with a rug.

"Is your special permit still on the windscreen, Axel?" asked Dietrich as he set the car in motion. "We don't want to be stopped anywhere, and we certainly don't want to be searched."

Axel nodded, pointing towards the impressive-looking pass that he'd affixed to the window earlier. "Just focus on getting the hell out of here," he said impatiently, "and leave everything else to me."

"You never told us how you came by that," observed Kristina, her hands shaking as she pulled the car rug more securely over Heike's limp form.

Axel made no reply, simply muttering directions to Dietrich from time to time. Heike, only barely conscious, could hear their voices as if at the end of a dark tunnel while they discussed what they should do. She felt the car moving and lapsed into unconsciousness again as they sped down the winding streets. Following Axel's instructions, Dietrich drove at a furious pace towards the outskirts of the city, the tyres screaming in protest as he rounded the bends at high speed.

"Slow down, Dietrich," begged Kristina in a panic. "We don't want to attract any unwanted attention."

"All those months of planning... I could murder that silly cow," muttered Axel through gritted teeth."

"You probably have," observed Kristina dryly, as she lifted the rug briefly and glanced at Heike's deathly white face.

Axel ignored her as he traced a suitable route on the map. "Once we've crossed the checkpoint, I think our best bet is to head for Grünewald Woods. There are a lot of hiding places there, so from Heerstrasse, take Teufelseestrasse, then we'll look for somewhere to get rid of Lotte's little friend."

Kristina looked at him curiously. *He really is a cold fish*, she thought to herself as she bent down to have another closer look at Heike, who lay still and unmoving on the back seat where she had been thrown.

As they entered the thickly wooded district known as Grünewald, Dietrich turned down one of the narrower, less-frequented lanes. He was so preoccupied with finding an appropriate spot where they could safely dispose of Heike's body that he was unaware that a white Wartburg was tailing them at a discreet distance. He finally parked the car, and the two men dragged Heike out onto the ground and further into the trees.

"Is she dead?" grimaced Kristina, looking down at the inert form, the deathly pale face half-buried in leaves. The once bright curls were streaked with dirt and blood.

"She is now," replied Axel unemotionally as he fired a single shot into Heike's head. Her body shuddered as a stream of blood poured from a gaping wound in her temple.

Kristina could not repress a shiver at this cold, clinical dispatch of another human being, but before she could make further comment, there was a sound of a vehicle approaching down the grassy track where Dietrich had parked their car.

"We've been followed," hissed Axel. "Quick, into the car."

As Dietrich revved up the engine, the white Wartburg came into view only yards away.

"Hurry, Dietrich, hurry," cried Kristina, panic-stricken at the sight of the other vehicle so close behind them. "They're going to catch us."

Dietrich recklessly increased his speed, and their little car bounced and rattled along the bumpy ground, skidding as the wheels spun on the muddy track. He wove his way through the trees, trying to lose their pursuers. He glanced in the rear view mirror, momentarily taking his eyes off the track.

"Dietrich, look out!" screamed Kristina in terror as the small black car careered off course and headed at speed towards a large oak tree.

As Dietrich frantically wrenched the steering wheel round, the car smashed headlong into broad trunk. There was a moment's silence, and then flames shot from the bonnet. There was a deafening explosion and a ball of fire engulfed them. Axel, who had been thrown out of the car at the impact, could be seen half-running, half-stumbling through the trees, uncaring as to the fate of his erstwhile companions whose high-pitched screams could be heard from inside the burning wreck. A moment later, there was silence apart from the hissing of the flames.

Their pursuers clambered out of their vehicle and approached in a leisurely fashion. One of them stumbled over Heike's body as it lay half-buried in the leaves.

"Who's that?" he asked in Russian, kicking away the leaves from around Heike's face.

"That little red-haired woman we tailed a short while ago," replied his companion. "The silly cow should've listened to me when I warned her what would happen to her if she didn't go home. Some people don't have the sense they're born with, getting mixed up with that bunch and their madcap schemes."

With that, he bent down, scooped Heike up into his arms and carelessly threw her lifeless body onto the still smouldering car.

"What'll we do about him, Leo?" asked the driver as he joined the other two, indicating Axel's distant figure.

"We've been watching the lot of them for weeks. We know all their old haunts," replied Leo. "We can pick him up any old time. We'll consult with the boss when we get back to base."

"He wouldn't be best pleased if he knew we lost track of them for a while," observed his companion grimly. "Hope he never finds out, or our heads will be on the block."

Leo shrugged his shoulders. "I don't see why he should, and anyway, no real harm was done. They seem to have been too busy fighting amongst themselves to get up to very much."

With that, the three Russians walked back to their car and disappeared from view the way they had come. Heike's blackened body—by now unrecognisable—lay still smouldering in the flames as darkness fell.

Chapter 20

It was 2 a.m. before Maggie finished reading Heike's diary. She got up and stretched her stiff limbs before walking over to the window, reflecting on what she'd just been reading. The small flat she was now renting lay only a stone's throw from the Holiday Inn and was certainly not as plush as her hotel room had been but was cheap and pleasant and overlooked a quiet street. As she gazed out at the peaceful scene, she wondered how she would feel if she were now being watched by the occupants of one of those cars opposite her apartment.

She was too preoccupied with her own thoughts to see the man in wire-rim glasses watching her apartment from a doorway just across the street. She shook her head and grimaced before returning to her desk, once again picking up the slim volume that Marta had handed to her in the pub that evening. The moment she'd opened it, her heartbeat quickened as she realised that it was none other than Heike's personal account of her stay in East Germany, page after page covered in her neat, precise writing. She felt a thrill of triumph that perhaps she was actually getting close to the truth. Heike had obviously found consolation in recording the day-to-day events in Jena from the moment she had arrived.

I wonder why Marta didn't destroy it, Maggie thought to herself as she flicked through it. *Heike's made it pretty clear she suspected her involvement with the Stasi.*

As she began reading it more carefully, Maggie became totally absorbed in the intimate details of the other woman's everyday life. The further she read, the more insight she gained—not only into Heike's personality but also into the difficulties and dangers she was obviously facing. Her admiration for Heike's strength of character increased as she turned the pages and wondered if she would've had this inner resolve to withstand the daily menace of being watched and the threats and the manhandling that Heike had suffered.

"I would've been home on the first plane if I'd been in Heike's shoes, that's for sure," she said aloud.

There were also parts that she found hard to read. Heike's love for her husband and her bewilderment at his coldness towards her were recorded with heartbreaking honesty. Maggie felt she was intruding and that she should be skipping these pages, so intimate were the details of her physical relationship with Nicholas and their life together. Yet, the more she read and re-read certain passages, the more question marks kept surfacing, because the strange thing was that despite this closeness, she'd kept a great deal of her life in Oxford and Jena a secret from him.

"Perhaps, she was mixed up in something dodgy, and she didn't want him to know what she was getting involved in," Maggie murmured aloud. "That Lotte certainly seems to have been working on her. They obviously got quite close, which looks a bit suspicious."

She sat back in her chair and thought a bit, trying to get inside Heike's mind. It could be that because he'd predicted that she would have difficulties, she was too proud to admit the trouble she'd got into and so lose face. It was possible that for the first time in her life, she had really wanted to stand on her own two feet and follow her own wishes. Nicholas came across as an being overprotective and very controlling personality. Maggie shared a certain fellow-feeling with Heike as far as that was concerned and couldn't repress a giggle at Heike's very accurate assessment of some of her husband's shortcomings.

It was while she was studying the last two weeks of entries that Maggie felt a particular tingle of anticipation, sensing that here were real clues as to what might have happened to Heike. She started reading more carefully, making notes as she went along. The very detailed description of her involvement with Lotte's family now showed the importance that Heike placed on being drawn into these plans. Maggie frowned—it seemed a scheme fraught with difficulties. How could they have been sure that Heike would be given the opportunity to read such a speech or even present it just as a petition? It was as if she'd been groomed to be a target in some way and would end up as the fall guy, being blamed for some criminal act carried out by others. What Maggie couldn't understand was why Heike had got so close to Lotte in the first place and had continued to visit her when it was clear that it was only increasing the danger she was in. One answer lay in the penultimate entry where Heike had written:

I don't really want to get caught up in this, but I should support Lotte. She's the only person who's really made me feel welcome here. I'm not certain she's being completely honest with me, though. Perhaps, I can find out more if I stay close to her.

Heike also clearly felt a very strong loyalty to her country and saw East Germany as a bulwark against Fascism and Capitalism.

Maggie was surprised. *She was a much more political animal than I was expecting*, she thought to herself as she re-read bits of the diary again. Her discussions with Lotte had obviously struck a chord. She turned back the pages to some of the earlier entries where Heike described the bitter rows and recriminations she and Nicholas had had over the sufferings the Germans had inflicted on the Russian people during the Second World War. It had without doubt been a bone of contention. Perhaps, there were cracks in the marriage, after all.

"He seems to think we're all Nazi sympathisers," she had written rather sadly, *"and that we were all equally guilty. Doesn't he realise we suffered, too? I believe he hates my country."*

There were also references to Jutta, who Heike seemed to view as a friend with whom she found a lot in common as a fellow East German. Jutta's role in all this puzzled Maggie. Was it really conceivable that a former girlfriend of Nicholas would promote the well-being of a woman who had taken Nicholas away from her? But it was the last entry, dated 6th October 1989, which had been written in a hurry and with some agitation that gave Maggie the most pause for thought. On this day, she at last poured out all her doubts and fears about the whole enterprise, and her final sentence sent a chill down Maggie's spine.

"I leave tomorrow, and I'm really afraid. Axel has made such threats against Nicholas if I don't cooperate. What if he should be murdered because of my stupidity? I have to go through with this, but I believe I'm going to die soon. If they try and tell you it was an accident, don't believe them."

Here, then, was the ultimate clue as to why she had not pulled out. Maggie picked up a photo of Heike lying on the desk beside the diary. Sue had given it to her to aid her in her search. Maggie studied it thoughtfully. The blue eyes stared out at her—obviously Heike in happier times. How pretty she was with her heart-shaped face and bright auburn curls, thought Maggie wistfully. She felt she had come to know her intimately and had shared her innermost thoughts, which had not been communicated to anyone else for reasons best known to herself. She sighed and closed the diary, rubbing her tired eyes, unsure as to what her next move should be. She was certain she was on the verge of a significant breakthrough, but realistically, she could not make any more progress without speaking further with Marta. Getting the other woman to open up further might not be an easy task.

However, it proved easier than she had thought. She found Marta in the student canteen, sitting in a quiet corner by a window, writing a letter. She nodded, unsmiling, when she saw Maggie. "I guessed you'd be looking for me, wanting to know more."

"I'll just get a coffee," said Maggie, relieved. "Then I'd really like you to fill me in on all the information you have on Heike's movements."

When she returned, Marta began talking without any further prompting, "Heike got herself involved with a really nasty self-seeking group. Lotte, who drew her in, acted as the bait, presenting a soft, harmless side to their activities. They'd done their homework well and knew Heike's weaknesses—how to touch a chord with her, how to put pressure on her. As you've probably realised after reading her diaries, Heike was introduced to Lotte through Jutta who had her own axe to grind in getting her so-called friend involved in what was to prove a very dangerous enterprise."

Maggie was wide-eyed at this. "You mean Jutta hoped that Heike would get killed?"

"Well, perhaps not that, but certainly to get picked up by the authorities, and thus removed from the scene. When I notified the Stasi that she'd been visiting Lotte, I'd no idea what they were planning, and it was only afterwards that I realised I should've done more to warn her off," she paused. "She really was an innocent abroad and very vulnerable. I've blamed myself ever since she disappeared. Jutta was part of a Stasi cell in Oxford in the early days, you know," she added almost as an afterthought.

Maggie's eyes opened wide. "Oxford! You're joking, Marta!"

"I'm not. Oh, come on, Maggie, you're being naïve. Think of all the spying activities in Cambridge during the Cold War."

"Do you know who else was involved in Oxford?"

"No, and I wouldn't tell you if I did," Marta replied crisply.

There was a brief silence while Maggie absorbed all this. "So, what exactly was Heike involved in?" she said slowly. "And how did you find out?"

Marta looked at her with a glint of amusement in her dark eyes. "You really have led a very sheltered life, Maggie. It must be the dreaming spires that protect you from the real world. Perhaps, I should first explain the family setup which was actually part of quite a large subversive political group that didn't necessarily always have the same aims. This particular small cell consisted of Lotte's son, Dietrich, and her daughter-in-law, Kristina, and, in particular, Axel, who was the hard man of the group and had political ambitions. Their plan was twofold—one was to get rid of Mielke and Honecker, whom they saw as tired old men incapable of steering East Germany in the right direction, so that the administration might have more appeal to its population, and the second was to eliminate Gorbachev, whom they saw as a threat to the viability of the country, though I'm not sure if Lotte knew what their plans were for Heike."

Maggie gasped. "You mean assassinate the Soviet President?"

"Exactly, and Heike was a useful tool in that scheme—someone to push the blame onto while they escaped. By the way, did you know Kristina was Jutta's younger sister? She would've had a lot of sympathy for her attempt to win Nicholas back, so Jutta had no difficulty in persuading them to support her idea of implicating Heike. Everyone was satisfied."

Maggie was so flabbergasted with all of this that she could hardly get the words out. "No, I didn't know that, but how did you find out all of this?"

Marta chose her words carefully. "The Stasi and the KGB were cooperating. We didn't learn the full story until Lotte and Axel were picked up and questioned. As it is, I still don't think we've got the complete story by any means. It was a very dramatic time politically, and I wasn't part of the interrogation team. That wasn't my job, so I can't really tell you much more I'm afraid."

Maggie shook her head in disbelief and sat in silence while she absorbed all that she had been told. "Are Lotte and Axel still alive?" She hardly knew how to phrase this, "I mean, were they…" She trailed off, uncertainly.

"Eliminated?" continued Marta, looking faintly amused. "No, they're still alive as far as I know. They were probably interrogated for several days or weeks, put into solitary confinement and deprived of sleep and if that didn't work, then I'm sure some other form of persuasion would've been used," she added dryly.

Maggie shivered; it was a world she could barely comprehend, and yet, Marta was so matter-of-fact about it all. "Do you know where either of them might be?"

Marta thought for a moment. "Possibly. I could trace Lotte, because the Stasi took her in, but Axel was tracked down by the Russians, and his trail's gone cold. The three KGB men who snatched him were the ones assigned to shadow the whole group in Berlin on the day of Gorbachev's visit. They lost sight of them for a couple of vital hours, and so, were sent back to Moscow to be disciplined— probably in the Gulag by now!"

"Did you ever get to meet them?" asked Maggie curiously.

Marta shook her head firmly—she was certainly not going to divulge her brief liaison with Leo at a time when she was at a very low ebb. She recalled an evening of knocking back one vodka after another and then some joyless, brutish sex. She shuddered at the memory—no, she certainly didn't want to relive that evening. She drained the remains of her cold coffee. "I'll see if I can hunt down Lotte," she said lightly, "but I'm making no promises."

And with that, Maggie had to be content for the time being at any rate. She felt a certain satisfaction, however, at her success so far. She had certainly achieved a lot more than Nicholas, she reflected, as she made her way back to her flat and smiled at the thought momentarily before remembering how they had parted.

Chapter 21

Nicholas fumed with impatience as he waited in the Vice Chancellor's office. He glanced at his watch; yet another late start to a meeting. The last few weeks had been full of frustration. Despite his best efforts, he had been unable to extricate himself from the numerous meetings and seminars that always plagued the life of the academic staff at the end of Trinity Term. Unlike the vast majority of students who vacated their rooms and departed for gap years, study tours or temporary jobs to support their ever-growing bank loans, their supervisors were forced to remain for a month or more—winding up the remains of the past academic year and preparing for the next.

Ever since he had discovered Maggie's plans, Nicholas had been racked with anxiety. He was only too aware of the dangers she might face in a country still coming to terms with the revelations emerging from the newly released Stasi files. Those who had spied on their family and colleagues were probably living in daily fear of disclosure of their past activities and were not likely to welcome questions on highly sensitive issues such as the disappearance of the wife of an Oxford professor. He had no real idea of what she was planning to do and no way of contacting her. Repeated phone calls to her London flat resulted merely in a BT call-minder response, and Nicholas could only assume that she had already left. The meeting this afternoon was one of the last, and he determined to set off at the end of the week.

Urged on by Sue, John had gone round to see him one evening and had tried to dissuade him from making this trip, saying that he was wasting his time on a wild goose chase.

"But look, Nicholas, if you're determined to go, I've got some leave coming up next month. Why don't the three of us go together?" he suggested persuasively. "It'll be nicer for you to have some company, and Sue and I could do with a break."

Nicholas shook his head firmly. "Nice idea, John, but no, thanks. Now, if you'll excuse me, I've got work to do."

He looked at his watch again. The meeting should have started ten minutes ago. He was just considering leaving a note pleading another appointment when the Vice Chancellor bustled in, full of profuse apologies for keeping him waiting.

"You know how it is at this time of the year, Nicholas. So many people saying they just want a minute of your time. We'll try to keep this brief, shall we?"

Nicholas smiled grimly, hoping that he would be true to his word. However, it was an hour later before he was able to make his escape. He hurried up to his study to deal with a few last minute tasks. As he opened the door, the telephone started ringing. He grimaced and picked it up resignedly, praying that it wasn't a colleague demanding some vital piece of information.

"Nicholas Stowkovsky."

"Nicholas, thank God, I've got hold of you at last. I've been trying your mobile, but there was no response."

"I've been in meetings all day, I've had it turned off. James, whatever is the matter?" Nicholas hardly recognised his brother-in-law's voice. He was normally so calm.

"It's Alex," replied James, his voice breaking with anxiety. "She's got breast cancer. She noticed a lump a couple of months ago and…"

"Why didn't she tell me?" interrupted Nicholas, shocked and surprised. He and Alex were so close, he couldn't believe she hadn't confided in him.

"I think she couldn't bear to face up to it, and also, she didn't want to worry you unnecessarily before we were both sure. At first, we thought the lump was benign, but a biopsy has revealed a cancer. Any chance you could come and see her? She's eaten up with worry, I know."

All thoughts of Maggie and the difficulties she might be facing vanished from his mind as Nicholas contemplated the awfulness of losing his beloved sister. The blood thumped hard in his throat. "How bad is it?" he said urgently. "Don't keep anything from me. I want to know."

"It doesn't look good." James's voice was a pale shadow of his normal confident tone. "She has got to have a mastectomy, and we don't know yet whether the cancer has spread. The problem is that Alex didn't go and see the medics as soon as the lump appeared. She just kept pretending that everything was all right—didn't even tell me at first. You know how she is—she never wants to admit anything's wrong with her." His voice broke off with a half sob.

"If there's any chance of your coming up, I know it would do Alex the world of good to see you."

Nicholas broke in, "You don't even need to ask, James. I'll be up on the first flight. I'll ring as soon as I'm about to board the plane out of London. Give Alex my love and tell her I'm on my way."

As he flung a few things into a case, Nicholas reproached himself for not seeing more of Alex. Yes, they spoke regularly on the phone and emailed each other, but their physical contact had largely been restricted to vacation time. This was determined partly by the distance between Oxford and Edinburgh and partly by Nicholas's absorption in his academic life.

That's what probably lost me Heike, he thought bitterly. *My damned work— that'll be poor comfort if I lose both the most important women in my life.*

As he sat on the plane, he shut his eyes, recalling memories like miniature snapshots of him and Alex together—orphans—a product of the violent times that had torn their family apart. Their Aunt Eliza, who had welcomed them so kindly into her family in Edinburgh, gently told the bewildered youngsters of their mother's death. The nine-year-old Alex had later put her arms round his neck and whispered, "We must look after each other now, Nikko." Nicholas felt his eyes sting with tears at the memory.

His brother-in-law was waiting for him as he emerged from the baggage hall, carrying his small suitcase. James, who was usually rather taciturn and not prone to showing his emotions, grasped Nicholas's hand with extra warmth. "It was good of you to come so quickly," he said gruffly.

"As if I wouldn't," Nicholas replied, looking at him anxiously. "Where's Alex? Is she okay?"

"She's resting," James said as he led the way across the carpark. "Her operation's tomorrow."

The forty-minute journey seemed endless as Nicholas fretted in silence, torn between impatience and anxiety. Finally, James pulled up outside a substantial grey stone house on the outskirts of the city. Alex had obviously been on the lookout for the car, and the front door opened almost immediately.

Nicholas bounded up the few stone steps, and Alex flung her arms round his neck. "It's so good to see you, Nikko."

Nicholas held her at arm's length for a moment, studying her pale face with concern. His sister was tall and dark as he was, and no one seeing them together could have mistaken them for anything other than brother and sister.

"How are you, my Alex?"

His sister smiled a wide, bright smile. "Fine, fine." Then almost immediately, uncharacteristically, she burst into tears, burying her face against his broad shoulder. Nicholas wrapped his arms around her, murmuring soothing words, while James carried his suitcase upstairs, tactfully leaving brother and sister together.

Afterwards, looking back on this episode in his life, Nicholas recalled only the all-pervading anxiety suffered by those who see a loved one being wheeled away for surgery. He had to restrain himself from begging the surgeon to take good care of his sister. Only later, when he and James knew that Alex was going to make a full recovery did the normally abstemious Nicholas allow himself to be persuaded by his brother-in-law to head to the nearest pub where they both downed several large glasses of whisky in celebration. How they got back to the house, he could not remember.

Alex enjoyed her husband's account of their unsteady walk home enormously and teased Nicholas when he came to visit her, carrying a large bouquet. "Just think what your students would think of their staid professor, rolling home drunk in the early hours." she said mischievously.

Nicholas looked rather shamefaced for a moment and then laughed as he sat down beside her. "Not so much of the staid, Alex. I still have my moments, you know!" The thought of his last meeting with Maggie came suddenly unbidden to his mind, and his face reddened and clouded over.

Alex studied him keenly. "I think you're hiding something from me, Nikko."

"Now's not the moment," he said, forcing a smile. "You just concentrate on getting yourself better."

She did not let the matter drop, however, and on her return home, she pressed him further. Reluctantly at first, but unable to resist her persistent questioning, he finally poured out the whole story, including his growing feelings for Maggie and the arrival of that dreadful letter. It was a welcome relief to unburden himself at last.

Alex remained silent for a few minutes when he had finished and then said slowly, "I think you should follow Maggie to Germany as soon as you can and see if she has managed to discover anything further. My guess is, Heike's dead, but if you're able at least to solve the mystery of her disappearance together and find out what she was up to, it'll put a closure on that part of your life, and you can make a fresh start."

Nicholas studied her face carefully. "You really think this, Alex?"

"I definitely do, Nikko. I'm well on the mend now, so don't waste any more time. Promise me." She pressed his hand encouragingly.

Nicholas nodded slowly. She was right, he knew. He couldn't rest until he had tied up some of these loose ends. This had to be the final push, the final effort, whatever it might reveal.

Chapter 22

Although he was now impatient to get to Jena, Nicholas had decided to go by train. It would give him thinking time undisturbed by telephone, e-mails or simply someone tapping on his door. As the night-sleeper clattered its way across Europe, he lay in his couchette and reflected long and hard on what he was now forced to admit were probably the final years of his marriage. What were the real reasons why Heike had wanted to take this study leave? Perhaps their relationship had become shaky sometime before, and he'd just been too busy to notice. As he tossed and turned, unable to sleep, he was forced to recognise, finally, that Heike had not been completely satisfied with their life in Oxford.

She'd always wanted to travel more and many times had urged him to take early sabbatical leave. But for him, the academic life of the university was all-consuming, and Nicholas, ever mindful of promotion and his heart set on the ultimate prize of a professorship, had continually temporised. Afraid of losing her, he had jealously guarded her, being overprotective and casting a damper on her occasional spurts of independence. However, the niggling fear that refused to go away and kept resurfacing was that possibly, they'd not been really suited to one another at all.

He had been well aware of her parents' doubts about their marriage—it might well be that the scars of childhood had gone too deep for the two of them to contain their deep bitterness over what had happened during the war and its aftermath. Among the thoughts that whirled into and through his head was the overriding suspicion that his wife had been leading a double life. He remembered those papers he'd found in her drawer, and his doubts came crowding back. He recalled the many times Heike had gone out for the day and how evasive she'd been about what she'd been doing.

"I'll be thinking you got a boyfriend soon, darling," he'd said jokingly on one occasion. She had flushed and told him not to be silly, but had still refused to be drawn into revealing anything. He reflected bitterly over his careless assumptions that she'd always be there for him regardless. "I said some dreadful things about East Germany sometimes," he murmured aloud. "She cared deeply about her country, I know, and I just steamrollered over it all." Perhaps, because of the way he'd been over the years, she'd become fed up with him and their life together and had got drawn into some sort of undercover operation or other.

Nicholas recognised that he could be impatient and was prone to a quick temper. He knew he had been on a particularly short fuse since Heike's disappearance, and that had certainly not helped him either with Maggie or some of his other students. *I drive everyone away who cares about me*, he thought ruefully. At least his sister understood how he was feeling. At the memory of his last words with Alex before his departure, his harsh features softened. Sue and John had proved to be such a support, too.

"Thank God for understanding, long-suffering friends," he mused. "I don't deserve them."

At Leipzig, he prepared yet again to change trains for his final destination and realised that he had still not decided how to handle matters if and when he managed to track Maggie down. It was nearly eight weeks since her departure from Oxford, and his assumption that she was still in Jena might prove to be false. He was not even sure what he would say to her if he did meet up with her and fervently hoped that a flash of inspiration would come to his aid at the appropriate moment. The taxi dropped him off at the hotel he had booked before leaving Oxford and where he had stayed on previous visits to Jena when he had come looking for Heike. Not much had changed, he thought ruefully, looking round at the faded wallpaper and shabby furnishings.

After a quick shower, he set off on the short walk to the university, but when he asked for help in locating a Mrs Maggie Stewart, he drew a blank. The unsmiling, severe-looking clerk at the Enquiries desk greeted his request frostily and remained impervious, not only to his not inconsiderable charm but also to the revelation that he was an Oxford professor. He was able to extract only that Maggie had signed up to do some personal research, but she refused to divulge even whether Maggie was still on the campus. Old habits of secrecy die hard in East Germany, thought Nicholas ruefully as he stood outside in the early evening sunshine, trying to decide what his next move should be.

As he strolled rather aimlessly round the town, he kept an eye open, more in hope than expectation of glimpsing Maggie among the crowds of people hurrying home after work. He thought how shabby and sad-looking they appeared, so unlike their West German compatriots—rather like their city, which seemed no more entrancing than the last time he was here. Unfortunately, the bombing of 1945 had destroyed much of the ancient part of the town and only one or two remnants of its ancient past remained. The unsightly blocks of flats did not improve the general impression of a place still rooted in its Communist past.

Yet, he mused as he retraced his steps, so many East Germans still hankered after those days of national identity, instead of being swallowed up as they were now by their more dominant neighbour. How many of those who had fled though the open border crossing, sobbing with joy and craving freedom, had actually found a better life? Nicholas was only too well aware of the lingering memories and festering resentment in his own country after Gorbachev opened the floodgates to the freedoms that led to the disintegration of the Soviet empire. The old terrors were often forgotten in nostalgia.

Maggie, blissfully unaware of his presence in Jena, was busy following up some of the leads she had gleaned from Heike's diary. Marta hadn't yet got back to her after their last meeting, so she decided to do some scouting around on her own. She tried to retrace Heike's steps as far as possible by locating Heike's old apartment—in a grey, featureless 'Plattenbau'—a typical, unattractive East German apartment block of the 1960s. She walked from there to Lotte's house in Torgasse. It was dark and gloomy just as Heike had said. The shutters were firmly closed, and the whole building looked as if it had been unoccupied for some time. Feeling she had nothing to lose, Maggie knocked at the house next door. The woman who answered it—grey and featureless as the house itself—was obviously unwilling to divulge much information about her erstwhile neighbour.

"They came and took her away one night more than two years ago, and I haven't seen sign or sight of her since," was all she was prepared to say.

When Maggie asked whether anyone else was in the house at the time, she simply shrugged her shoulders and closed the front door firmly in Maggie's face. Steeling herself for another rebuff, Maggie tried the neighbour on the other side and found the elderly lady there rather more forthcoming. She invited Maggie in and offered her a cup of tea.

She confided that she and Lotte had been quite friendly. "Until that son and daughter-in-law moved in with her… then, she became rather withdrawn—a bit afraid of them, if you ask me. But we're talking about some time ago, and I can't remember all the details."

"Did anyone else come to the house during this time?" asked Maggie.

The old lady paused a moment, screwing up her faded blue eyes almost lost in a network of wrinkles. "There seemed to be a lot of comings and goings—usually youngish folk and some foreign-looking." Then she lowered her voice so that Maggie had to lean forward to catch what she was saying. "One night, there was a right old hullabaloo—a couple of official-looking cars drove up, and there was a lot of shouting and screaming inside the house. We, all of us, drew our curtains—we didn't want to get involved."

Maggie tried to visualise the scene. "So, you didn't get to see what happened? She asked finally.

"Oh, no!" the old lady looked quite shocked. "They were dangerous times, you know. It didn't do to poke your nose in; you could never tell who was informing on whom."

Maggie cast a glance round the shabby little sitting room as she took her leave. She guessed that this frail little lady, like so many East Germans, was leading a hand-to-mouth existence. There were certainly not many signs of Western affluence here. She resolved to pop back one day soon with a basket of fruit and some chocolates perhaps, as a thank you for the tea.

She strolled back to the university, feeling a little disconsolate. She appeared to have come to a dead-end, unless Marta was able to give her any more information. If she could only track down Lotte, assuming she was still alive, she perhaps could shed some more light on Heike's movements.

* * * * *

After three days of prowling round the university campus, Nicholas's patience was finally rewarded when he spotted Maggie on the other side of the road near the student canteen, chattering to a group of fellow students. She looked thoroughly at ease. She always seemed to have the knack of blending in wherever she found herself, he thought rather enviously. She somehow looked different, too—her hair was cut in a sophisticated bob, its fairness lightened by the sun. Nicholas felt his heart stop for a moment, and then he was filled with a combination of overwhelming joy and relief that she was safe.

He realised with a sense of shock that he had fallen in love with her gradually and unwillingly. Perhaps that letter had deadened his feelings for Heike as he faced the idea of her being part of a spy system, perhaps betraying him or their friends in Oxford while occupying a trusted position there as his wife. Maggie's presence in his life had, over recent months, become more and more important to his sense of well-being. This love had crept up on him and refused to be ignored, however strongly he'd tried to deny it to himself. He would have liked there and then to have rushed up to her and to put his arms around her while he poured out his feelings. It took only an instant before he came to his senses, and with a wry smile, he realised that with the memory of their last meeting, Maggie was hardly likely to have welcomed this impetuosity, particularly in the middle of a busy street.

Maggie crossed the road, deftly dodging between the cars roaring up the hill, swinging her briefcase and totally unaware of his presence until a familiar voice made her swing round.

"Hullo, Maggie. I've finally tracked you down."

As he reached out to take her heavy bag, she jumped back, drawing in her breath, her eyes both startled and hostile. "What are you doing here?"

It was not an auspicious start, and things did not improve as he tried to put into words his anxiety about what she might be drawn into.

"I'm perfectly capable of looking after myself. Why don't you go away and leave me alone to manage my own affairs?" retorted Maggie, rather nettled by what she felt was his patronising manner.

"Because it happens to be my affair as well," snapped Nicholas, his temper rising. "Heike was my wife, and this has nothing to do with you. I don't know what you're doing here, anyway, meddling in my affairs. It's none of your damn business."

"You can't bludgeon me anymore, Professor Stowkovsky, as you used to! We're not in Oxford now," exclaimed Maggie, equally angry.

Her icy formality made him step back. He was handling this so badly. He tried a more conciliatory tone. "You've caused me, all of us, a lot of anxiety just going off like that. Now, I'm here in Jena. You can at least bring me up to date with anything you've managed to find out and let me take over while you get on with your studies."

Maggie was not to be so easily won round, however. "Don't talk down to me; you're being patronising. I've achieved far more than you were able to, and I'm not handing any information over to you so that you can cut me out. I was perfectly alright till you turned up."

Before long, they were rowing furiously in the middle of the pavement. The passers-by eyed them curiously—the tall, fair woman shouting at her companion, whose dark hair seemed to be bristling with rage as he waved his arms in his anger, giving vent to occasional Russian expletives. They parted around them, giving the pair a wide berth. Just as abruptly as the argument had started, they both stopped, and Maggie suddenly began laughing. Nicholas glared at her for a moment before reluctantly joining in.

"What a spectacle we're making of ourselves," he grimaced. "Let's find somewhere quieter to continue our conversation in a more adult way, and perhaps you might reconsider a sharing of knowledge so that you can fill me in on what you've discovered, if anything."

Maggie was ready to bridle again at what she felt was a rather dismissive assessment of her efforts, but she realised that he was offering an olive branch and that he really did have the right to know what she had gleaned.

After she had left her bag in her locker at the university, they made their way to the Botanical Gardens, dominated by the Planetarium Zeiss. Having found a quiet seat, Maggie then told Nicholas all that she had discovered both from her contact with Marta and also from her visit to Torgasse. When she had finished, Nicholas looked at her for a minute in silence, recognising a new air of confidence about her. To his relief, she appeared to have forgotten their last, highly charged meeting. In this neutral environment, she certainly didn't appear to find him as awe-inspiring as she had in Oxford and was talking to him much more as an equal.

It must be difficult, he thought, for mature students coming up to Oxford and getting to grips with all that was required of them in a relatively short space of time. He couldn't resist a wry smile as he recalled that she'd told him to shut up at one point during their argument. Since he had become a professor, he couldn't remember the last time someone had said that to him. And she'd certainly been a lot more successful than he had in extracting information.

He realised she was looking at him expectantly. "You're not afraid of me anymore, are you, Maggie?" he asked unexpectedly.

She looked at him for a second and, seeing the warmth in his dark eyes, flushed and looked down at the ground. "No, I'm not, but I don't know what that's got to do with what I've been saying."

Nicholas smiled at her, and she looked away again, suddenly embarrassed. "You've accomplished so much, Maggie, that I don't know where to start. I'd obviously like to see the diary and to speak to Marta. She was very uncommunicative with me before, but perhaps, with the two of us chatting with her, we might get more out of her."

Maggie shook her head in a manner which brooked no argument. "No. I'd rather keep the contact just between her and me for the moment. I think I've got her confidence. We don't want her clamming up. The diary is another matter. As Heike's husband, it's yours by right. It's in my briefcase at the university. I'll drop it off at your hotel if you let me have the address."

He frowned. "No, I'm not happy about this, Maggie. How do you know you can trust Marta? As a former Stasi agent, you don't know what she might be up to. Old habits die hard. You could be in some danger if you keep on questioning her."

Maggie got up. "I'm sorry, Professor Stowkovsky, but this is non-negotiable. You might frighten her away. I'll obviously keep you informed as to what's going on, but I don't want to be mollycoddled. I can look after myself."

With that, Nicholas had to be content. They walked back to the university in stony silence, and Maggie turned down his invitation to dinner, saying kindly but firmly that she had work to do. Though inwardly fuming, he realised there was no point in having another row, though as she turned away, he privately resolved to keep a close eye on her. He could not resist a parting shot, however.

"I do think Professor Stowkovsky is a little formal under the circumstances, don't you, Maggie? I'm sure if you try hard, you'll find that Nicholas is not too difficult to say!"

With a brief wave, he was gone before she could think of a suitable response.

Chapter 23

On the Sunday morning after her meeting with Nicholas Stowkovsky, the telephone rang. Maggie, who had just stepped under the shower, cursed under her breath. She padded across the sitting room, her bare feet leaving a trail of wet footmarks, the towel trailing behind her.

"Hope I didn't get you out of bed," Nicholas's crisp tones greeted her as she picked up the receiver.

"I was showering actually," said Maggie tartly, wrapping her towel more securely round her wet body. She shifted the receiver from one damp hand to the other. Trust Nicholas to catch her off her guard. Despite her irritation, as she pictured him, dark hair ruffled, probably pacing up and down in his usual impatient way, her heart missed a beat at the sound of his voice.

He continued as if she had not spoken, "I thought we might have dinner tonight. I've found quite a decent Gasthof just round the corner from my hotel—shall we say 7.30?" His tone assumed her agreement.

"I've got a lot to do today. I'm not sure I've got the time." Maggie strove for some show of independence. "It's very kind of you, Professor Stowkovsky."

"It's Nicholas, not Professor Stowkovsky. For goodness' sake, Maggie, don't be ridiculous." His voice brooked no argument. "Surely, we've moved on from all this formality by now. Anyway, there are some important things I want to discuss with you, and the phone's not the place. I'll pick you up about 7 p.m."

Maggie flushed at the amusement in his voice. *He's the absolute limit*, she thought. She was half inclined to continue arguing but doubted if she would win this battle. He was just as likely to come around and bang on her door this evening.

"I'll meet you there if you give me directions," she said finally, with some attempt to be self-assertive. "I may have to go into the university later."

Nicholas hesitated but finally conceded. "It's the Gasthof Muller in Schillerstrasse. I'll see you there at 7.30." Without waiting for her response, he put the phone down.

"I could cheerfully ring his neck at the moment," Maggie said aloud as she padded back to the bathroom.

Gasthof Muller was almost full and buzzing with activity by the time Maggie arrived. She had decided to be a little late on purpose in the hope of making him anxious and was prepared with explanations about having a lot to do and the tram being late. However, Nicholas, who was seated at a corner table beside the window, looking very relaxed, did not even glance at his watch but merely rose to his feet and kissed her briefly on both cheeks.

"You look very nice," he said approvingly, holding out her chair.

Maggie blushed as she thanked him. She had spent most of the afternoon trying to decide what to wear from her rather limited selection of clothing. She had finally decided on a pale grey linen trouser suit and a red silk shirt.

"I'm sorry I'm late," she said. She glanced round the little restaurant. Every table was now occupied. "You were lucky to get a table. It's obviously very popular."

Nicholas poured her a glass of wine. "Oh, they kept this one by the window for me," he said carelessly. "Is this okay for you, Maggie? You prefer red, if I remember correctly, but we've got a bottle of white on order."

"No, no, that's fine." Maggie sipped her wine appreciatively. She glanced across the table at Nicholas, who was busy looking at the menu. He was the sort of man for whom waiters would always keep a table, she thought. He had that quiet air of dignity and authority that commanded respect. He had dressed with extra care tonight, she reflected; a compliment to her, perhaps. She studied his face thoughtfully, a myriad of emotions were racing through her head. She was experiencing a conflict of feelings which disturbed her. She should still have been angry with him but somehow the hurt and bewilderment she'd felt at Oxford seemed to have evaporated.

He glanced up from the menu, catching her unawares, and smiled at her as if reading her mind. The warmth in his eyes made her feel suddenly shy. "You look thoughtful, is it something you want to share?" He stretched out his hand and rested it on hers.

She shook her head, embarrassed and confused, and pulled her hand away. To her great relief, he moved on to the subject of ordering their dinner. The waiter bustled over immediately once he saw that Nicholas was ready to order. His German was faultless, Maggie noted, but then, he had been married to Heike for many years. Her heart sank as she remembered Heike's journal and the love she'd expressed for her husband. She then realised to her annoyance that she had completely forgotten to call into the university to pick up the diary on her way to the restaurant. She had spent so much time thinking about her clothes and then agitating about what he wanted to say to her that it had completely slipped her mind. *I should be focussing on Heike*, Maggie reproached herself, *not having dinner with her husband, kidding myself that I'm not falling in love with him.* She resolved to be more distant and businesslike from now on.

This proved difficult, however. Nicholas was a good host. The wine flowed and the dinner was excellent—fresh asparagus served with ham and cheese and large jacket potatoes. This was followed by freshly made ice-cream, a speciality of Gasthof Muller, and large cups of steaming, fragrant coffee. The other diners were laughing and joking, and as the sounds of jollity from the other tables increased, it was hard to be standoffish. Maggie found herself unwinding in the convivial atmosphere as she and Nicholas talked in the easy, relaxed way that Sue's hospitality had fostered all those months ago. She even found herself using his first name inadvertently, and his lips twitched, though he made no comment. Their waiter arrived at regular intervals with steaming platefuls of food and Maggie, half-laughing and half-protesting, accepted second and third helpings.

"You'll only hurt their feelings if you refuse," Nicholas advised her, helping himself to large spoonfuls of Hollandaise. "The chef views it as a personal insult if you don't finish all they bring."

"That's absurd, Nicholas," Maggie chuckled as she took another sip of the Riesling that Nicholas had ordered. *I'm getting a bit tipsy*, she realised, but somehow it didn't seem important at that moment.

That's better, Nicholas thought to himself as he watched her visibly relaxing and her increasing enjoyment of the evening. She had been like a coiled spring when she arrived, as if she was still wary and afraid of him, or of her own feelings, perhaps. He considered her thoughtfully. She was becoming so dear to him, but he was afraid of frightening her away if he made his feelings too plain. The way she had drawn back from him made him only too aware of how on her guard she was. Still, at least she was using his Christian name. He had let it pass, afraid of embarrassing her, only too relieved that that was one little barrier overcome. Later that evening, Maggie could not recall what topics they had discussed, only that they had seemed so in tune. The only subject carefully avoided was Oxford with all its associations and ramifications.

It was not until their coffee finally arrived that she rather belatedly recalled that there was a reason for their meeting. Nicholas, who had been talking about the improved skiing facilities in Aviemore, became aware that she had become abstracted.

"Am I boring you, Maggie?" he teased as he refilled her cup.

She flushed and stiffened a little. "No, no, of course not, but I think there was something you wanted to discuss and also, I've got an apology to make. I forgot to pick up Heike's journal from the university this evening. It is safely locked away, though."

"Don't worry, let me have it when you next go in," he sighed. The magic moment had passed and he once again had to face the reality of the task that lay ahead. He had considered confiding in Maggie about the accusations in the anonymous letter but decided against it for the present. There was something of far greater concern to discuss.

"Have you spoken to Marta yet about the matter we talked about the other day?"

"I left her a note, but she hasn't come back to me, and I haven't had time to follow it up. Anyway, I don't want to hustle her. She may clam up altogether." Maggie felt on the defensive.

"I'm not trying to hurry you," Nicholas spoke gently, "but I wanted to warn you to be careful when you do finally catch up with her."

Maggie looked at him with startled eyes. "What are you suggesting? You think Marta could be a danger in some way?"

"It's possible," Nicholas spoke in guarded tones, aware of other diners in close proximity. Though with the noise everyone was creating, it was unlikely that their conversation could be overheard. "I've been doing a little unobtrusive research into Marta's background. Those like her have things to hide that they don't want to become public property. It's in their interest to protect themselves at all costs."

"But she's spoken to me so openly," Maggie protested, "almost as if she wanted to unburden herself."

"Perhaps that's the impression she wanted to give in order to get you to reveal what you were up to." Nicholas spoke in a matter-of-fact way, but his words sent a chill down Maggie's spine. "When people are trapped, they hit out; believe me, I know. These former agents can't afford to be exposed. They might even kill to prevent that. You're straying into areas you've little or no experience of, and you must be on your guard."

"On my guard for what?" Maggie felt her unease growing.

"People watching your apartment, the same car outside for several hours. Check that you're not being followed—just keep your eyes open." Nicholas wondered if he was frightening her too much, but perhaps it was better that way than her sleepwalking into some trap.

"I'll be really careful," said Maggie in a small voice, mulling over what he had just told her. She found it hard to believe that Marta could be so duplicitous, but perhaps it was rather unlikely that she should reveal her story to a perfect stranger if there had not been a hidden motive. After all, she thought to herself, why should Marta befriend her in particular when she had kept quiet for so long? Perhaps, she had been rather naïve in assuming it was all so straightforward. She now felt rather foolish to think that she had been so trusting.

Nicholas studied her troubled face. "You're not alone in all this, you know, Maggie," he said comfortingly. "We're working together, and I'm sure we'll solve the mystery of Heike's disappearance somehow."

Maggie nodded, feeling some reassurance, but the evening had lost its glow, and it was with some relief that she saw Nicholas ask for the bill. As they left the little Gasthof, she could not prevent herself from glancing around to see if any suspicious figures were lurking in the shadowy doorways. The little streets where she had been walking so fearlessly suddenly seemed full of hidden menace. She would have been even more concerned if she'd noticed the man with wire-rim glasses just across the street. He was partly obscured by a newspaper kiosk, making a call on his mobile, his eyes fixed intently on the two of them.

Nicholas, seeing her instinctive movements, drew her arm in his. "I'll walk you home," he said firmly, "and try not to worry or let your imagination run away with you, or I'll wish I hadn't warned you at all. There aren't desperados waiting to jump out at you from every corner, you know. You're perfectly safe in these well-lit streets. Just be on your guard, and don't go wandering around on your own late at night in some lonely part of the town."

"Try not to worry!" exclaimed Maggie indignantly. "What do you expect after all you said to me in the restaurant just now? You're impossible."

"That's more like it," said Nicholas approvingly. "Much more like the Maggie I know, and incidentally, you look lovely when you're angry," he added, smiling down at her.

Maggie flushed and pulled her arm away from his, refusing to enter into any further conversation during the walk back to her apartment block. Nicholas insisted on seeing her up to her own door. Maggie knew that he was hoping that she might say something to break the ice, but she simply held out her hand and thanked him for the dinner before closing the door firmly behind her. It was only after he had gone that she wished she had been more conciliatory and rushed to the window to call out to him, only to see his tall figure disappear round the corner.

Chapter 24

After the warnings that Nicholas had given her the night before, Maggie found it hard not to keep glancing out of the front window to see if her apartment was being watched. A sudden movement in the courtyard below made her start. She then realised it was only Frau Borkmann, her neighbour, walking her little brown dachshund, and felt rather foolish. However, when she left for the university, she still found herself looking around from time to time to check if anyone was following her, but nobody seemed at all interested in her movements. She was too inexperienced to realise that she was being tailed the whole time by a professional well-skilled in hiding his activities and waiting only for instructions as to what his next move should be.

As she waited for the tram, she reflected that Heike must have suffered that same sense of insecurity of looking constantly over her shoulder to see if a shadowy figure was lurking in a doorway as she passed by. In a strange sort of way, she felt as if she was taking over Heike's persona and reliving her experiences. It was a spooky sensation.

The university corridors were shady and peaceful after the bright sunshine and the bustling streets outside the campus. Most of the students were probably either at lectures or already working in the library. Maggie walked briskly through the cool stone hall and past the reception office, mentally reviewing her programme for the day. She remembered her promise to Nicholas the evening before.

"I must pick up my briefcase first," she shifted a pile of library books from one arm to another, "and afterwards see if I can find something to wrap up Heike's diary. I can then walk round in the lunch hour and deliver it at the hotel reception as we arranged."

She turned left towards the room where the students' lockers were housed. In the dim light of the passageway, she saw that the door leading into the locker room was wide open.

"Good, no need for me to get out my passkey," she said aloud. "Another student must be in there already."

As she approached the doorway, someone suddenly emerged. Maggie paused for a moment, her heart beating faster. She sensed that there was something not quite right here. There was a furtiveness about the movements of this figure muffled in dark clothing on such a warm day that aroused her suspicions.

"Hey, wait a minute!" she shouted. "What are you doing?"

She started to run down the passageway. The intruder, obviously startled at being observed, stopped momentarily and then charged towards Maggie at breakneck speed. Maggie gave a little whimper of fear but bravely stood her ground for a second, trying to see if she could recognise who it might be, but whoever it was had taken the precaution of wearing a hooded jacket. It was impossible to see if it was male or female. As the figure drew level with her, she tried to use her books as a weapon but was pushed violently against the wall by a strong hand. Taken by surprise, Maggie completely lost her balance and fell heavily to the ground. She lay there, winded for a moment, her books scattered around her. The incident lasted barely a few seconds, but Maggie noted that her attacker, now speeding away from her, was carrying a small package. It was only a fleeting glance, but a sudden fear gripped her.

She struggled to her feet and hurried into the large, windowless room lined with grey lockers. All were closed, except one—her own, its door swinging wide open. On the floor lay her briefcase with all her possessions scattered over a wide area as if the thief had shaken it violently in a hurried search. Maggie bent over to look inside it. The diary which had been securely locked in one of the inner pockets had vanished. The lock had been forced open. She frantically rummaged around in her case with trembling hands to no avail. She searched through the remaining contents of her locker, but nothing else seemed to have been disturbed. The thief had known exactly what to look for.

She repacked her briefcase and then stood for a moment, unsure as to what she should do next. *I can't ask the porter at the reception about someone carrying a small package*, she thought. *Too many embarrassing explanations would be needed.*

Although she had taken every precaution to keep the diary safe, she felt so responsible for the loss. Whatever was she going to say to Nicholas? He would be angry, and rightly so.

However, he was surprisingly understanding when she phoned him. "You couldn't have known this would happen," he said comfortingly. "Wait for Marta to contact you, but it might be better not to tell her anything about this. Then, when we next meet, we'll discuss it further." With that, he rang off. He stood for a moment, deep in thought, his face grave. Although he'd tried to reassure Maggie, he was now seriously worried. "Why on Earth did Marta give the diary to Maggie in the first place? Was she trying to entrap her in some way?"

He began pacing up and down, trying to work out what might be going on. "There's something very strange here," he muttered aloud. "What's Marta up to?" An idea suddenly struck him. "There must have been material hidden in that diary that someone didn't want discovered, something they didn't think Maggie would spot but perhaps I would. My sudden arrival on the scene must've taken them by surprise, so they had to get the diary back somehow." He felt a cold chill in the pit of his stomach. That meant he and Maggie were being watched. Maggie was in danger; he was sure of it. "That's decided it," he muttered. "The sooner we leave here, the better for her." The diary and its contents suddenly seemed of little importance compared to Maggie's safety.

Maggie, relieved that Nicholas had not blamed her in any way, tried to put the whole episode out of her mind, but after his warnings in the restaurant and now this unexpected theft, she felt very much on guard. Every street seemed to hold a hidden menace. She just hoped that it would not be too long before Marta came back to her with some information.

It was several days, however, before Marta contacted her, and Maggie had been getting more and more edgy, fearing that something had gone wrong or that Nicholas might pop up at any time to check up on her progress. To her relief, a rather terse message in Marta's familiar scrawl finally arrived in her pigeonhole, suggesting they meet that evening for a drink at their usual pub.

"I've managed to track Lotte down," Marta greeted her. "She's in Leipzig, in an old people's home. Here's the address." She pushed a piece of paper across the table.

Maggie was a bit taken aback. "Aren't you coming with me?"

"I don't think she'd be very pleased to see me." Marta was brisk and to the point. "She probably blames me for the group's demise." She gave Maggie a few brief directions and seemed unwilling to talk about the matter any further.

After saying goodbye to her, Maggie caught a tram and then strolled back to her apartment in a thoughtful mood. Marta had changed in her manner towards her, had become rather cool and unfriendly. It puzzled Maggie. It was as if she resented Maggie's continual questioning. She wondered if it was wise to go alone to see Lotte after all that had happened. Despite her defiant words, she was of half a mind to invite Nicholas to come with her. She remembered all his warnings to be very careful where she went. Perhaps, she was stupid to go wandering off on her own. However, it was a simple enough journey, which didn't involve travelling to any particularly dangerous suburbs.

She told herself firmly that there could be no risk in visiting an elderly lady in an old people's home, and anyway, Lotte was far more likely to respond to a woman without a male presence which might seem more threatening to an old lady. She resolutely thrust from her mind unwelcome memories of Heike and parallels with her taking similar risks which had then led her to danger. This was an undertaking she really wanted to carry out independently of Nicholas and show him that she was not afraid to carry on her investigations alone. She visualised reporting to him in triumph after her visit there and presenting him with some concrete results. These more pleasant thoughts helped stiffen her resolve.

Chapter 25

I can think of worse places to wind up in if I'm old and alone, thought Maggie as she wandered along the tree-lined drive to the long, low, ivy-covered building that lay ahead of her. The mellow bricks gleamed in the early afternoon sunshine, and she could see some of the elderly residents relaxing in the comfortable chairs dotted around on the grass. Marta's directions to this 'Altersheim' had proved simple enough to follow, and the matron had been very welcoming over the phone when Maggie said she wanted to visit.

"You may find her mind wanders a bit, my dear," she warned after she had greeted Maggie in her office. "She doesn't always make a lot of sense. But I'm sure she'll be pleased to see you. She doesn't get many visitors these days—her only son died in a car accident, you know."

"How dreadful!" exclaimed Maggie, horrified. "When did this happen?"

The matron was vague. "I don't really know the details. That's all we were told when she was brought here."

She seemed to want to avoid further questions and led Maggie out into the gardens to where a tiny, shrunken figure was sitting in a wheelchair beside a small lake, gazing vacantly across the water to where a few ducks were squabbling over some bread.

"I've brought your English visitor, Maggie Stewart, to see you, Lotte," the matron informed her cheerily before hurrying away, leaving Maggie to hover uncertainly, wondering whether the old lady was aware of her presence. She didn't even glance in her direction, though Maggie finally pulled up a chair and sat down close beside her. There was a long silence while Maggie stared at the ground, rather nonplussed. Then, she realised that Lotte was looking at her—her gaze was faded and rheumy, but still, Maggie recognised the sharp, beady little eyes of Heike's description.

Her thin, reedy voice seemed to come from a long way off. "I don't know you. Why are you here?"

"I'm a friend of Heike's," Maggie said. Not strictly true, of course, she realised, but easier than a long complicated explanation. "We've all been very worried about Heike," she continued, "and would like to know what's happened to her."

The old lady looked at her suspiciously. "Heike never mentioned a Maggie to me—how do I know who you are? Anyway, Heike's gone and she's never coming back." Lotte gazed out over the lake again.

"You mean she's dead," Maggie said bluntly, feeling that Lotte was drifting away from her once more.

The small dark eyes looked vague. "Perhaps, who knows? She went to Berlin and didn't return, then they came and took me away." Her eyes became fearful. "They keep you in solitary, you know, lights on, and bang on the door if you try to sleep. In the end, you tell them anything…" her voice trailed off.

There was another long silence. Lotte seemed in another world, her lips were moving, but Maggie could only make out one or two words—names and places that she didn't recognise. "Poor little Heike," Lotte murmured as tears ran down her wrinkled cheek. "Poor little Heike."

"Tell me about Heike," Maggie insisted, trying to fix the old lady's attention once more.

"They raped me, those Russians. Have you ever been raped?" Lotte asked abruptly.

"No, no, of course not," stammered Maggie, quite shocked and taken aback by the sudden turn of conversation. The old lady had lost her completely; she wasn't making any sense at all. Maggie didn't quite know how she ought to respond. Lotte had closed her eyes tightly, as if she was trying to obliterate some nightmarish experience.

The minutes ticked by, and Maggie felt that she should be making some sort of response. "What happened to you? When was this?" she said finally.

Lotte opened her eyes again. "The Russian army came through our town in '45. All us women suffered the same—like animals they were. As I lay on the ground, one of them on top of me, another unzipping his trousers as he waited, the others, about eight of them, stood around and drank and laughed. I could hear screaming all round me. When they'd finished with us, they all moved off into the next town, taking everything they could lay their hands on." She broke off suddenly, the pain of the memory etched in her face.

Maggie was transfixed with horror at what she had just heard. She had read accounts of this, of course, but hadn't ever experienced it at first hand. She reached out for Lotte's hand and took it gently in hers.

Lotte looked at her as if seeing her for the first time. "We loathed the Russians, all of them—still do. I'd have killed that Gorbachev myself if I'd been able—coming here and telling us what to do." She had become very agitated—her face flushed and her hands trembling. "That's what we wanted to do, get rid of him, but it all went wrong." She put her hands over her face.

Oh no, what do I do now? Maggie thought. *This is all my fault.* She could see tears running down Lotte's face and started to get really concerned. She got up to call one of the nurses. At that moment, Lotte suddenly seized her hand and pulled her down beside her again. Her long, claw-like fingers pressed deep into Maggie's flesh with surprising strength.

"Those Russians chased my son and little Heike to their deaths, and Kristina—they're all dead."

"When was this? Where did it happen?" asked Maggie urgently.

But Lotte was tiring and drifting away and made no attempt to reply. She gazed at Maggie with sad, vacant eyes still wet with tears. "All dead," she repeated. "Car crashed into a tree."

"But where?" asked Maggie again. "Try and remember."

"Some woods," mumbled Lotte, "near Berlin." She fell silent again. She muttered a name and Maggie leant forward. It sounded like 'Grune'.

"Did you say Grune?" she asked.

The old lady looked at her, and Maggie thought she glimpsed a recognition of that name, but there was no point in persevering, Lotte had closed her eyes and appeared to have drifted into a deep sleep. As Maggie got up to leave, a nurse came to wheel Lotte back to the house.

"It's time for her supper," she explained.

Maggie watched them go—her mind racing over what she'd just heard. It seemed almost certain now that Heike was dead, if she could rely on the wanderings of a confused, elderly lady. But elements of Lotte's story had rung true and fitted with other parts of the jigsaw that Maggie had been piecing together. How had Lotte discovered all this? Someone must have visited her and broken the news. But Lotte had also been taken by the Stasi. Could they have told her? But if that was the case, then surely Marta would have known, unless she was keeping something back for fear of incriminating herself.

Maggie's thoughts whirled round and round in circles as she tried to piece together Heike's last hours. She wondered if she should question Marta again. How would she react to further probing? Wouldn't it be worth the risk though if Marta could shed a little more light on some of the things that were still puzzling her? She didn't know what to do for the best, but even so, she'd found out a great deal and achieved a lot of what she'd set out to do. She felt pleased with herself and was looking forward to sharing all of this information with Nicholas and showing him what she could achieve on her own.

As Maggie walked back to the station, she reflected sadly on the vulnerability and fragility of the civilian population when exposed to the meaningless violence in the aftermath of war. Lotte's bald, almost matter-of-fact description of her horrendous experience was an account that had been retold many times—perhaps even to Heike—but still lacked none of the horror in the retelling. The individual suffering and the acts of brutality that lay behind this story had really shocked Maggie. As she sat on the train back to Jena, she gazed unseeingly out of the window and thought about poor Lotte and her family. They had possibly been instrumental in Heike's demise, but the acts of barbarism that Lotte had experienced would no doubt have had lasting effects.

The emotion and fear on both sides had generated a savage need for retaliation. The ideology and lack of morality that had characterised this stage of the war had stemmed from even more brutal actions inflicted by the Germans on the Russian civilian population. Thus, it had become almost a point of honour to cause the same level of misery.

What puzzles me, she thought, *is this ideological romanticism on the part of people like Lotte—this clinging to an outdated repressive Communist ideal which needed Russian support to maintain it. Damn Nicholas*, she murmured ruefully, *I'm even beginning to think like a bloody prof now*. She couldn't repress a half-smile as she imagined discussing the part his country had played in supporting the East German regime. Quite a good argument that might be!

What was quite clear, though, was that by 1989, Gorbachev had realised that the Communist vision had nothing left to give, and for this, Lotte's group had determined that he was to pay with his life. Those who either could not or would not recognise that communism offered only deteriorating living standards and little hope, thought that by assassination they could underpin the failing East German administration.

Maggie realised with a start that the train was pulling into the station at Jena. As she walked back to her apartment, she wondered what her next plan of action should be. "I'd better make contact with Nicholas tomorrow," she decided. "Let him know what I've found out, then perhaps a trip to Berlin might be a good idea."

She felt now that she was in the final stages of solving the mystery, though whether she would ever discover Heike's final resting place was another matter entirely.

Lotte, now safely ensconced in her room, was speaking querulously on the telephone. "You've got to come over as soon as possible. I've had another visitor. The nightmare is starting all over again." With a shaking hand, she put down the receiver without waiting for a reply.

Chapter 26

Nicholas remained silent for several minutes after Maggie told him all she had learnt from Lotte, though she kept back a few of the more personal details. She was not sure what his reaction would have been to the behaviour of some of the Russian soldiers. What Lotte had revealed more or less confirmed all that Nicholas had feared, of course, but that made it no easier to finally realise that Heike was dead, possibly at the hands of one of his own countrymen. Maggie tactfully left him to his own thoughts and wandered off to look at some of the newly planted borders in the Botanical Gardens where they had agreed to meet. Actually, she was relieved to have some moments to herself. When they had met earlier at the entrance to the gardens, he had taken hold of both her hands, and before she could pull them away, he tried to apologise for his behaviour in Oxford.

"I wanted to say this the other day when we first met, but it didn't seem the right moment, we were too busy arguing." He grimaced at the memory. "And the other night at dinner, I still couldn't find the right words or the appropriate time."

He would have said more, but Maggie, who had crimsoned at being reminded of that violent embrace, mumbled that it was forgotten as far as she was concerned and walked away from him down the path towards a convenient seat close to an old stone wall and far enough away from any curious ears. Nicholas had no alternative but to follow her.

"I'm really sorry about Heike's diary," Maggie said abruptly, when they were seated, trying to break the awkward silence. "You must blame me for not keeping it in a better place."

"I can't bear recriminations, apart from those applied to myself." His smile was forced. "You mustn't blame yourself. You weren't to know that someone might try to steal it. Now, tell me what you've found out."

He really was a surprising man, Maggie thought, as she wandered up and down on her own. You never knew how he would react—sometimes gentle, sometimes abrasive. She reflected that Sue was probably right when she'd told her that Nicholas was in love with her. That thought made her feel awkward and joyful at the same time. She knew she was attracted to him, but it was easier to be standoffish and keep him at arm's length while she examined her own feelings.

"I don't know why I should be in love with such a disagreeable and overbearing man," she declared defiantly to a small bird sitting on a branch above her head. It twittered at her before flying off to join its mate. Yet, he had been so charming the other night and was obviously concerned about her safety. She had repaid him by being grumpy. Maggie sighed and resumed her stroll.

When Nicholas eventually joined her, they sat down again on a seat nearby, and he asked her what she thought they should do next. The fact that he was actually asking rather than informing her emboldened Maggie to suggest that they should plan to go to Berlin.

"I had thought at one time of involving Marta," she continued hesitantly, "but after what you said the other night, you'll presumably say that's not a good idea."

"No," Nicholas said firmly, "it most certainly is not. You and I will go together. I don't want a former Stasi agent tagging along under any circumstances. Even if you think you can trust her, I do not."

Maggie felt a quick flash of anger—he really was an impossible man. It really didn't matter what she wanted or thought. She might have guessed that the old Nicholas was still lurking behind that deceptive façade of seeming compliance. "I've done all the leg work here. My ideas should be considered," she replied hotly.

But Nicholas would brook no argument. "I'm going and she's not, and that's that," he snapped. "You can come or not as you choose."

Looking at his face, which had darkened as it always did when he was angry, Maggie saw that she would have to give in gracefully or risk another bruising confrontation. To her irritation, she realised that he had more or less assumed her acquiescence and had started making more concrete plans.

"We'll leave in about a week's time, and in the meantime, you can see if Marta has anything further to tell you that would be useful—for example, more details about this Grunewald area that Lotte referred to," he told her in a condescending way that made her seethe. He smiled blandly. "But remember, she's not coming with us, and also be careful what you tell her about our movements."

When Maggie finally caught up with Marta and told her what Lotte had said, Marta looked at her thoughtfully before asking her were her plans were now.

"I want to follow up this reference to Grunewald, perhaps go out there sometime and explore a little and try to piece together what might have happened to Heike," Maggie told her, thinking it more politic not to mention Nicholas. "Do you know where exactly Lotte might have meant? I've had a look at a map and it looks a pretty big area."

She thought that Marta did not look best pleased. "It's obviously Grunewald," she replied rather sharply, "but you're right, that's an enormous area—why don't you let things rest now and go back to England? You've found out what you came here for. What's the point of ferreting around anymore?"

But when Maggie insisted, she reluctantly drew a brief sketch map showing the relative position of Grunewald to Berlin and marked the most important parts to visit. "It'll be like looking for a needle in a haystack trying to discover anything there," she warned dismissively. "Apart from all the wooded areas, the lakes are very extensive. There's even a beach—it's very popular in the summer with Berliners. You really haven't a hope of finding anything; you'll be wasting your time."

Seeing how determined she was, Marta made no further attempt to dissuade Maggie, who was relieved that she did not suggest accompanying her. She would have had an awkward time trying to find an adequate excuse to put her off. Marta seemed to have no answers concerning the other things that were puzzling Maggie and was obviously unwilling to discuss matters further. She became more and more terse the further Maggie probed, and she decided not to question her further. In light of what Nicholas had been saying to her, the other woman's attitude rather disturbed her. She had been so forthcoming before. It was as if a veil had come down through which Maggie was not permitted to pass. She was glad to bring their conversation to a close.

Marta then simply asked Maggie to be sure to let her know when she was leaving so that they could have a last drink in their favourite bar. In fact, Maggie decided not to see her again before leaving Jena as there seemed little to be gained by talking to her anymore. She felt she could always use the excuse of having so many things to do before setting off. Mindful of the warnings that Nicholas had given her, she therefore simply left a quick message on Marta's answerphone giving only a vague idea of her plans and saying that she would keep in touch.

A couple of days after her meeting with Marta, she left the university, swinging her briefcase and feeling quite pleased with the progress she was making in her research. She glanced across the road and saw her tram pulling up on the other side of the street. There was no traffic in sight, so she dashed across, waving her arms to catch the attention of the driver. As she did so, a car, which had been parked a few yards away, suddenly pulled out when she was halfway across and accelerated at full speed towards her. Maggie spotted it out of the corner of her eye and, as if hypnotised, froze momentarily in the middle of the road like a startled rabbit before sprinting even faster towards the safety of the pavement. The car caught her only a glancing blow but sent her spinning across the road, leaving her in a crumpled heap, stunned but not seriously injured.

"Du blöder idiot," exclaimed a passer-by, shaking a fist at the fast disappearing car as it sped away with tyres squealing as it rounded a corner and disappeared from view. He then rushed over to where Maggie lay in the road, and a small crowd quickly gathered. Maggie was helped to a chair in a nearby café, where a glass of water was brought to her.

"These young fools deserve to be locked up," said the proprietor, looking at Maggie's white face with concern, "I'd better call the police and an ambulance."

"No. I'd rather you didn't do that. I'm fine," said Maggie shakily, "but perhaps I could use your telephone to call a friend of mine who will come and collect me."

She prayed that Nicholas would be in his hotel room, and she almost burst into tears of relief as she heard his familiar tones.

"Accident! Where?" his voice sharpened with anxiety. "I told you not to go wandering off Lord knows where."

"I didn't, I haven't," Maggie said quickly. She briefly explained where she was and what had happened.

"Are you all right?"

"I'm fine," Maggie reassured him quickly, "but could you possibly call for a taxi and come and collect me?"

Within ten minutes, a taxi was outside, and Nicholas was striding into the café. Maggie's remaining entourage watched with interest as he bent over her and took both her hands in his.

"Are you injured, Maggie? Have you seen a doctor?" He looked closely at her face where a livid bruise was already appearing on her temple.

"I'm only shaken up; really, Nicholas, no broken bones or anything, but I just want to get out of here." Her voice quivered as she got rather shakily to her feet. "Please take me back to the apartment."

While he was leading her out of the café, one of the onlookers tapped him on the shoulder and said confidentially, "It was deliberate, not an accident. I saw it all. The car went straight at her. The problem is that it was all too quick, and none of us got the number."

Nicholas nodded his thanks, and his face was grave as he sat beside Maggie in the taxi. He glanced at her drawn face and decided not to share his fears with her. This was something he had better keep to himself, he thought, there was no point in scaring her. He dropped her off at her apartment and made sure she was comfortable and not in serious pain.

"I want you to promise me that you'll stay put until I come and see you tomorrow," he said firmly, "and be sure to let me know if you have any problems, whatever the hour."

"What sort of problems?" Maggie said anxiously. She had been relaxing on the rather lumpy sofa where Nicholas had insisted she should rest. She winced as she sat up suddenly.

"I mean, if you start feeling any serious pain," he quickly manufactured a reason for his firmness.

"Right," said Maggie, not entirely convinced, "I promise."

With that, he had to be content. He was not happy leaving her there alone and hoped she would be sensible.

"We must get out of this town as soon as possible," he decided as he made his way back to his hotel. "Before anything worse happens."

Chapter 27

Maggie slept only fitfully that night. The painkillers she had taken before going to bed helped her to doze barely an hour or two. Her left hip, which had taken the full brunt of her fall, throbbed, and her whole body ached. She could not find any position that was comfortable and now, in her wakefulness, had a chance to reflect on what had happened to her. A terrible fear took hold of her, which she could not shake off, that this had been no accident, but a very real attempt on her life.

At one point, she eased herself out of bed and limped over to the window to see if anyone was outside watching her apartment. However, the street was silent, with only the occasional car cruising straight past. She still could not rid herself of the conviction that out there, someone wanted her removed. She now longed to escape from the town where she had earlier felt so secure and relaxed. The trip she and Nicholas were planning could not come soon enough.

The night seemed endless, and when the sky finally lightened, and the first rays of sun shone in through her bedroom window, she decided to have a shower to occupy her mind. She stood naked in front of the bathroom mirror and examined her injuries in the full light of day. She had extensive bruising all down one side of her body and her temple was now a bright yellow. She felt herself over carefully but nothing appeared to be broken. She had been extremely fortunate. The cold shower was, for once, welcome, and she felt more refreshed and considerably brighter compared with an hour ago.

When Nicholas called around as he had promised, he was relieved to see that she was moving around with relative ease. Her facial injuries still gave him cause for concern, and he looked closely at the rapidly spreading bruise on her temple. Although he was anxious to get away from Jena as soon as possible, he wondered whether she was really fit to travel.

"I still think you should let a doctor have a look at you," he said, "just as a precaution."

"No, I'm fine, really," Maggie assured him.

"Well, you have a quiet day here while I make all the necessary arrangements," he said to her firmly. "If you don't promise me that at least, I shall lock you in and take the key!"

Maggie laughed and agreed reluctantly. "But I want some say in what we're doing."

He just nodded and, with a brief wave of his hand, was gone before she could say any more. With this, she simply had to be content. She now once again felt too tired and shaky to concern herself with what Nicholas might be up to and decided to take his advice and rest.

"One thing I won't do is tell him all the things I was worrying about last night," she murmured to herself as she tried to make herself comfortable on the lumpy sofa. "He'll probably only laugh at me and tell me I've got an overactive imagination or something."

After a couple of hours, she grew bored and restless. The rest of the day stretched ahead with nothing to do. She didn't feel like studying, and her head ached too much. She got up and wandered around the apartment and then made herself a quick snack, but even this was just a brief time-filler. A glance at her watch showed her it was only two o'clock. *I feel trapped in this damn place*, she thought. At that moment, a sudden knock on the door made her jump. The noise of it seemed to echo round the apartment. "Who's that?" she asked shakily, her heart thumping. "Is it you, Nicholas?"

"Hullo, Maggie, it's me, Lisa, Lisa Borkmann. Are you busy?"

Maggie's body sagged with relief at the familiar voice as she opened the door. It was her neighbour from upstairs, one of the few people that Maggie had got to know from the other apartments. Lively and friendly, about Maggie's age, she was divorced and lived alone.

Lisa looked shocked at her appearance. "Maggie, whatever have you been up to? Have you had an accident?"

"Just a hit and run driver," Maggie said carefully. "I'm alright, really."

"Well, you don't look alright. I'd better go and leave you in peace."

"No, don't go. I could do with the company," Maggie said firmly. "Come and sit down and I'll make us some tea."

"Well, if you're sure," Lisa sat down reluctantly. "Actually, I've got a favour to ask you."

"Do you want me to look after Pickles?" asked Maggie as she came over with the tea. She occasionally took care of Lisa's little dachshund if she was going to be late home from work.

"No, no, nothing like that, especially not at the moment with you like that. You really ought to be resting, Maggie."

"I'm okay, don't worry." Maggie brushed Lisa's concerns aside. "What can I do for you, then?"

"Well, I know it seems a bit of a cheek," said Lisa rather embarrassed, "but I've got a special date tonight, and I was wondering if you'd lend me that lovely red jacket of yours. I know it's a favourite of yours. You wear it all the time. But I'll take great care of it. My best coat's at the drycleaners. I've just been around there and it's not ready yet."

"Is that all?" Maggie laughed. "Of course. You've lent me things many times. I'll go and get it. You're about the same size and colouring as me, so I'm sure it'll be fine."

When Lisa left clutching the scarlet jacket and still pouring out her thanks, Maggie said jokingly, "Don't forget, I'll want to hear all about it."

Lisa raised her hand in acknowledgement and Maggie was still smiling as she closed the door. Lisa's visit had done her a world of good.

Much to her surprise, Maggie fell asleep almost immediately that night. She awoke with a start, uncertain and disorientated in the haze of sleep and painkillers. She could hear a commotion somewhere in the building—shouting—and a woman's voice shrill with fear.

Whatever time is it? She thought, bewildered. She peered at the clock by her bed. It was midnight. She lay in bed, straining to hear what was happening. The noise that followed was barely human—a long wailing cry of sheer terror. Maggie froze, and then there was a long moment of silence followed by a door banging loudly and the revving of an engine as a car drove away at high speed.

Maggie got out of bed, shocked and afraid. She ran into the sitting room. From her second-floor window, she had a good view of the street. There was nothing to be seen. She then hurried into the kitchen and lifted the blind to get a better view. To her horror, as she looked down in the courtyard beneath her window, she could see a tangled mass of twisted limbs. It was a woman's body in a scarlet jacket.

* * * * *

Maggie was distraught when Nicholas called around the next morning, and she started pouring out the whole story as soon as he stepped in the door.

"Why on Earth didn't you call me?" He was both angry and afraid for her. "I told you to phone if anything happened."

"It was the middle of the night. How could I?" Maggie burst into floods of tears.

"Come here." Nicholas put his arms around her. "You can't blame yourself, Maggie. You couldn't have known what would happen."

"I'm responsible. I lent her the jacket," Maggie wailed into his shoulder. He held her comfortingly. Her body was shaking with long, racking sobs. "Now let's sit down and you try and tell me what else happened after the…" he chose his words carefully, "after the accident. I hope you didn't go down."

"No." Maggie dabbed at her eyes with a handkerchief. She felt ashamed of herself breaking down like that. "No, there wasn't any need to. The residents on the ground floor were already out there, and I could hear the sirens of the police and ambulance. To be honest, I was a bit afraid of going down."

They looked at each other. There was no need to say anything. They both knew that Maggie had been the intended victim.

"But why?" Maggie whispered finally. "Why me?"

Nicholas simply shook his head. "I've no answers, I'm afraid—getting too close to the truth, perhaps."

He sat there for a moment, deep in thought, while Maggie closed her eyes, trying to block out the memory of last night.

Nicholas finally broke the silence. "Have you seen anything of the neighbours this morning? What did they think had happened?"

"They said that Lisa was always bringing men back to her apartment, and perhaps her date last night knocked her about and she fell out of the window," Maggie said dully. "She lived up on the fourth floor, you see. She wouldn't have had a chance." She shuddered as she remembered the fear in Lisa's voice.

"Right, that settles it," said Nicholas firmly after a slight pause. "You're coming back to the hotel with me. I'm not leaving you here alone a minute longer. I'm sure there won't be a problem finding you a room near mine. Then I can keep an eye on you until we leave for Berlin."

In the past, Maggie would have bristled immediately at what she would have seen as his hectoring tone, but for now, the fight had gone out of her. She simply nodded meekly and got up to pack her case. She was too stunned by what had happened to argue and was only too thankful to leave.

Chapter 28

The first couple of days in Berlin had proved difficult. The atmosphere was strained, and Nicholas was edgy and abrupt. Although at first, he'd been sure the car incident was simply an attempt to injure and frighten Maggie and put pressure on her to return home, he was now convinced that it was a murder attempt that had failed. Lisa hurrying back in the dark had clearly been mistaken for Maggie with fatal consequences. Whoever it was, was deadly serious and would try again. They were obviously determined to stop her ferreting about anymore. He'd thought long and hard about the best way of setting off for Berlin and to throw the assassin, whoever he was, off the scent. A hire car delivered to the hotel carpark down in the basement might allow Maggie and him to slip away unnoticed. But he was still not sure whether they'd been followed or not, and it made him less inclined to be conciliatory.

Maggie, not knowing what he was worrying about, was preoccupied with her own anxieties and found him terse and unsympathetic. *He's probably as tense and anxious as I am*, she thought to herself, *I must try to be calmer and more understanding.* But he was testing her patience to the limit, and the camaraderie they'd built up over the last week or so appeared to have evaporated. All the old resentments came flooding back because, in the end, she'd had no say in the travel arrangements or when exactly they should leave Jena, and she inwardly fumed at the highhanded way he informed her that he'd booked a hotel and organised a hire car so they could drive to Berlin.

"It'll give us more flexibility," he told her. He'd no intention of worrying her with the real reason.

"He could've consulted me," she mused resentfully. "He's got me to thank for getting this far." However, she was only too relieved; he seemed as anxious as she was to leave Jena and fell in with all his plans.

As things turned out, Maggie had to admit that the car was far more comfortable than the train. They had set off just three days after Lisa's death, and she was still feeling rather bruised and stiff after her fall in the road. At least in a car, she could relax in peace and be carried to her destination with no effort on her part. Nicholas was disinclined to enter into any conversation, and so, she spent most of the journey dozing. He seemed to be focussed purely on his driving, but was in fact also keeping a sharp eye open for any car that appeared to be tailing them for any length of time. When they finally arrived in Berlin, Maggie could find no fault with the hotel Nicholas had chosen.

The Hotel am Zoo was situated on Kurfurstendamm. It was comfortable and had a good restaurant refurbished in the original, old German style. It was also very convenient for the exploration they had in mind. If Maggie had anticipated any awkwardness or embarrassment on arrival at the hotel, she needn't have worried. Nicholas simply checked in himself and then airily waved a hand in her direction, leaving her to make her own arrangements while he headed for the lift.

They had at least agreed by mutual consent to spend a couple of days wandering around the former eastern quarter of Berlin. This was not through any idea of tracing Heike's movements there, which would have been almost impossible, but more to try and sense the atmosphere of how it might have been for her. Now, of course, they could wander unhindered across the former checkpoint areas. They drove to Schloss Glienicke in Potsdam and strolled over Glienicke Bridge where spies used to be exchanged and also looked at the remains of the Wall and Checkpoint Charlie nearby, still manned with its old warning notices.

Though neither had given voice to their doubts, Maggie sensed that Nicholas felt as she did, that there was very little hope of finding where Heike might have died. In a sense, they were both trying to postpone the drive to Grunewald and the moment when they would have to admit defeat and accept that they had discovered as much as they would ever know about Heike's last days. To give up now, though, might leave regrets that they had not made the final effort.

As they strolled around the large, bustling city, there were some elements that Maggie remembered, but in many ways, Berlin was so very different from how it had been on her visit with Tim in 1980. Then, it was a city bitterly divided, and it had seemed very exciting and adventurous for them both crossing to East Berlin. She recalled the frisson when the border guards searched their vehicle for escapees as they passed back through Checkpoint Charlie. Maggie and Tim were free to drive away, of course, but the reality was grim for those trapped behind the menacing, squalid barrier which separated them from family and friends. At the time, it had made her think of a novel by Christa Wolf—'The Divided

Heaven', in which Rita, a young East German, sees her lover escape to the West, effectively ending their romance.

She smiled wistfully as she remembered. "Rather like Marta," she mused.

"What are you thinking of, Maggie?" asked Nicholas, amused. "You're miles away." He seemed more relaxed now, happy to have got Maggie safely out of Jena.

She flushed. "I was thinking of the last time I came here in 1980 with my husband."

Nicholas looked startled. "I didn't know you were married." He felt a sudden wave of jealousy. Why had he assumed there was no one else? Her obviously warm friendship with Sebastian, perhaps. It made him speak more bluntly than he had intended.

"Widowed," she said briefly. "He died in the Falklands War." She bit her lip; it still pained her to speak of it.

Nicholas, though secretly relieved to know she was free, felt that he had blundered rather clumsily. "I'm so sorry, Maggie," he said gently after a pause. "I know how it feels to lose someone you love."

He reached out as if to touch her hand and then drew it back. There was an awkward silence for a moment. Since that day in the Botanical Gardens, neither of them had referred again to their last disastrous meeting in Oxford, for which Maggie was profoundly grateful. Their eyes met briefly and she saw genuine sympathy and understanding.

"We've both lost someone we loved," he said finally.

She nodded in agreement and no more was said, but after that, she felt once more at ease with him, and the air had somehow been cleared between them. She no longer found it difficult to call him Nicholas, and although he had smiled when she stumbled over it, the old awkwardness was gone once and for all. He occasionally took her hand as they walked along, and it felt so natural that Maggie did not attempt to pull away.

The local tourist board had been very helpful in providing them with a wealth of brochures and maps of the Grunewald area, and Maggie and Nicholas spent one evening pouring over all the information, trying to decide what their plan of attack would be. They sat themselves down in a quiet corner of the bar and spread out one of the maps. As they bent over to look at it together, Nicholas glanced at Maggie and had to restrain a sudden impulse to reach across and touch her cheek with his hand. He then felt a pang of conscience that he should even be considering such a move at this moment when he ought to be focussing on their search. He took refuge in being brisk and businesslike to cover his embarrassment.

Maggie, fortunately, totally unaware of his confused feelings, continued talking about their plans for the following day. The Grunewald region was quite a complex one, covering an area of thirty-two square metres, with a string of lakes stretching from Spandau to Potsdam and dotted with castles and a number of wooded areas. The prospect of covering such a large region was a daunting one, and she was beginning to think that perhaps, Marta had been right.

Nicholas studied one of the larger maps thoughtfully and then consulted a guidebook. "It says here that Grunewald is dominated to the north by Teufelsberg—apparently, it's the highest point round here. According to this, you can walk to the top, and there is a spectacular view over all the forested areas right across to Lake Havel. It might be a good starting point."

"Where is it?" asked Maggie.

"Here." He stabbed a long finger on a spot just south-east of Spandau. "It's about three hundred and fifty feet to the top, so we should get a good overview of the whole area from the summit—how do you feel about climbing up there?" He looked at her challengingly.

"That's no problem," said Maggie indignantly. "I've fully recovered now, and I'm not quite in my dotage yet." Then she saw he was laughing at her and realised that he was pulling her leg.

"Good idea," she said firmly. "Then we can decide from up there what else we can do to narrow our search."

Chapter 29

It was a long, hot climb to the summit. The guidebook had warned that it would take about twenty minutes, but this was certainly an underestimate, Maggie thought, as she panted and puffed her way up the rocky path. However, she was determined not to complain and was quite relieved to hear Nicholas breathing heavily when they finally made it to the top. The view was definitely worth the climb and was truly spectacular as the guidebook had said. They seemed to be surrounded by a sea of green—some of the leaves browned by the searing heat of high summer. Beyond the woods down below, the intense blue of the Teufelsee mirrored the deep blue of the sky. From an airfield on the other side of the Havel, a small plane climbed steadily heading out towards Tegel.

"This is quite a spot," observed Nicholas, studying the view through his binoculars. "It's hard to believe this mini-mountain is an artificial creation built from I don't know how many cubic meters of rubble after all the bombing during the last war. Now it's used as an all-season sports facility." He passed the glasses across to Maggie.

"That forested area down there is crisscrossed by quite a number of roads," she said after a few moments, "and Lotte told me there was a car crash—she was really definite about that. The plot to assassinate the Russian President would quite probably have been planned for his trip to Berlin in '89, and it's feasible that if Lotte's son and his wife drove out of Berlin, they might've been followed and headed out this way, hoping to lose their pursuers. Lotte also seemed very certain that Heike was with them." She thought for a moment. "She mentioned the car hit a tree—they all burnt to death, she said." Nicholas winced, his face pale

"I'm sorry," Maggie faltered, "but we've got to try and pin down a likely area."

" I know, I know," said Nicholas through gritted teeth, "but perhaps I don't want to know that Heike died like that. I can't even imagine why she was in the car with the others in the first place. It's an absolute mystery how she got tangled up with that lot. Even what you recall from her journal doesn't fully explain it. I just don't believe that she couldn't have slipped away from Jena and escaped from it all if she'd really wanted to. In her heart of hearts, she must have really wanted to go along with them."

He turned away, his jaw tightened as he remembered that damned letter. Maggie felt a rush of pity—at least she knew how Tim had died: instantaneous, the War Office had said, and she had a grave: they'd shipped his body home with full military honours. Nicholas had nothing, only rumours and possibilities. He could be a very irritating, assertive man, but it had become apparent to her that beneath that aggressive exterior lurked a more sensitive personality and a deep hurt due to his traumatic past. She recalled that conversation with Sue, and as she gazed at him, she knew that she loved him.

She reached out and put her hand on his arm. "I'm so sorry," she said softly. "Would you rather stop now? We could go back to Oxford—see this as a closed book."

"No," he replied more calmly. "We're here, and we're going to see it through as far as we reasonably can. I think now we should return to the car and explore some of those wooded areas as you suggested." He didn't make a move, however, but continued looking down at the woods beneath them. "I'm in love with you, Maggie, did you know that?" he spoke almost conversationally as if he were commenting on the weather.

Maggie looked at him wide-eyed, unable to speak. Her heartbeat seemed deafening, and she could barely breathe.

"I suppose I've known it for some time," he continued, putting the binoculars back in their case. He didn't look at Maggie, who continued staring at him open-mouthed at the unexpectedness of this sudden declaration.

"But Heike," she managed to gulp out at last, "I thought you were so in love with her."

Nicholas didn't reply for a few minutes, just gazed across the treetops to the water beyond. "I believe I was," he said slowly. "I was head over heels in love with her—it was truly love at first sight."

Maggie felt her throat constrict as she thought of Heike's confessions in her diary.

"I suppose," Nicholas continued thoughtfully, as his eyes followed a bird skimming across the trees, "I suppose I took her and her love for granted and assumed she was happy, but a gulf seemed to open up between us. She began to get restless, and we argued over stupid things." His mouth tightened as he remembered.

"But all married couples argue," ventured Maggie, who was amazed at his frankness about his marriage.

"Yes they do," he agreed, "but not all of them face the divide of race and the bitterness of war crimes. Perhaps, Heike's parents were right when they advised us to wait awhile; perhaps we both had too much emotional baggage." He finally turned to look at her and she saw the pain in his eyes. "And she may have betrayed me." He took hold of one of her hands as if to give him courage and told her about the anonymous letter and the list of names. "You're the only person I've told, Maggie, apart from my sister," he concluded. "I couldn't bear anyone else to know."

There was a long silence while Maggie absorbed all this, "It's possible it was a fake," she said hesitantly.

"That's true, but we shall never know for sure, and it just killed something inside me."

He pulled her slowly towards him and rested his other hand on the side of her face, caressing it gently. When she did not draw back, he bent his head and kissed her very softly on the lips. The kiss lasted only a few seconds and Maggie, for the first time since Tim died, felt desire coursing through her veins. Nicholas saw the love in her eyes and would have kissed her again. Her first instinct was to respond and throw caution to the wind, but she resisted and drew back.

She looked at him shyly. "I love you, too, but I don't want to rush into any relationship. I'd like to take things slowly—we're only really just getting to know each other, and somehow, until we've finished here, it just doesn't seem right. Can you understand?"

Nicholas nodded and released her reluctantly. She was quite right, of course. This wasn't the time or the place; they had to focus on their task until their search was exhausted. "For once, I agree with you," he said, smiling at her.

Her eyes twinkled appreciatively. "That has to be a first, Professor."

He took her hand to help her climb down from the ledge where they were standing. "That'll probably be the last time I shall admit that, you little vixen, so make the most of it."

The climb down was just as exhausting as the ascent had been, and they slithered and scrambled down the slopes, holding hands and laughing like a couple of teenagers, both too light-hearted to notice the roughness of the steep track. When they finally arrived at the bottom and set off in the car again, the woods seemed even more extensive than when they had viewed them from the top of Teufelsberg. "You even get wild boar here," observed Nicholas, as they drove along, looking for a suitable parking spot, "so I suggest we keep to the main paths."

They parked the car in a small lay-by and started their exploration. "I'd no idea the Grunewald covered such a vast area," said Maggie despondently as they wandered down one of the many footpaths. "It seems an almost impossible task."

The forest was divided by paths and tracks and in places, the undergrowth was almost impenetrable—a haven for all the wildlife that inhabited it. It was cool and even damp in places, and shafts of sunlight slanted through the canopy above their heads, creating dappled patches of shade on the path ahead of them. After two or three hours of fruitless search, Nicholas glanced at Maggie. She looked pale and tired. She'd been marvellous, he thought, following him uncomplainingly down one path after another on a search that he was beginning to feel was doomed to failure. They had, by now, exhausted their rather meagre supplies of food and drink, and he decided they should head back to the city and return the following day. Maggie greeted his suggestion with relief—she was beginning to develop a thumping migraine and was longing for the cool comfort of her hotel room.

Over the next few days, they continued their search, exploring a different area each time. Sometimes, they met the odd walker, but the holiday season was drawing to a close, and most of the time, they appeared to have the forest to themselves. It was an exhausting, dispiriting activity. Some of the paths were barely tracks, and they focussed on these in the hope of finding a spot which could have lain undisturbed and unnoticed. But this meant forcing their way through tangled undergrowth, getting hot and scratched in the process. As they crossed and re-crossed the myriad of paths with little result, Nicholas, never the most patient of individuals, swore softly as his clothes became caught up yet again on brambles and creepers.

"Damn this place, it's like making your way through a jungle," he said irritably at one point, trying to disentangle himself from a particularly obstinate piece of undergrowth that had somehow wound its way round his leg.

Maggie, who, in the beginning, would have joked him out of his bad mood, now merely snapped back, "It's just as difficult for me, you know, and I'm not complaining all the time."

They continued their search in stony silence for another hour until Nicholas, having looked at his watch, took her hand. "Sorry to be such a bear," he said. "This is getting us both down. Let's pack it in for the day, and I'll buy you a drink to make amends."

Each day now followed a similar pattern. Every morning, when they returned to Grunewald, their quest seemed more and more fruitless. As they trudged down yet another winding path, Maggie glanced at Nicholas, his face drawn and tired. *This must be such a strain for him*, she thought, *with all the history of what's gone before. We can't go on like this*. She longed to shout out, "Let's stop now and go back to Oxford and get on with the rest of our lives." But she didn't feel that she could call a halt to their search until Nicholas believed he had done all he could to unravel the mystery of his wife's disappearance. So, she continued to trudge beside him, trying to complain as little as possible. At the end of each day, on their return to the hotel, hot and tired after another fruitless search, they would retire to the bar and examine their map to plan the sector for exploration on the following day.

As the days passed by, they became more and more despondent. It became harder and harder to work up any enthusiasm for the next day's trek when they seemed to be making so little progress, and the whole enterprise appeared to be a total waste of time. They were both tired and disappointed and became increasingly edgy with each other. While they sat having dinner after yet another day with little success and a lot of bickering, Nicholas looked at Maggie's downcast face and came to a sudden decision.

"I suggest we should make tomorrow our last trip out to Grunewald," he announced. "It's absurd carrying on like this. If we find nothing after that, then I think we should give up, accept we've got as far as we can and go back to England and get on with the rest of our lives together."

Maggie, startled at the unexpectedness of his words that so echoed her own feelings, spilt her coffee on the tablecloth. She dabbed vainly at the spreading brown stain with her napkin and poured herself a fresh cup. "Is this really what you want, Nicholas?" she said slowly. "You were so keen to unearth the truth—to find some sort of closure."

"I was, I am, but we can't continue like this, achieving nothing. It's putting too much pressure on both of us. It's just pointless. Let's make a final push tomorrow to find some sort of clue, and if nothing turns up, well, we can at least feel that we've done our best." He reached out and took her hand. "You agree with me, don't you? After all, we've only got Lotte's ramblings to go on. Perhaps, she made a mistake."

Maggie was silent for a moment. "If I'm honest, I can't deny that I'd be relieved," she said finally, "but disappointed, too. After all, Lotte seemed very sure." She sipped her coffee while she thought over what he had just said. She had wanted so much to find answers for him and now it appeared they would never really know. Nicholas was right, though; it really was pointless to waste their time on a wild goose chase. She sighed, "Okay, I agree, and we'll try to cover as much ground as possible as a final effort."

* * * * *

Next day was cooler and more overcast, and spots of rain appeared on the windscreen as Nicholas skilfully negotiated the busy roads and skirted round the city, heading down Bismarkstrasse into Kaiserdamm and finally into Teufelseestrasse and the Grunewald once more.

While Nicholas focussed on the driving, Maggie tried to recall all that Lotte had said to her. "What were the key phrases?" she mused aloud. "Lotte mentioned a car chase, they ended up in Grunewald, there was an accident very probably in the forest and the car caught fire."

"Perhaps, they drove down one of the tracks to throw their pursuers off the scent," suggested Nicholas as he overtook a slow lumbering lorry. "If it happened in one of the denser areas of the forest, a burnt-out wreck could lie undetected for years. Perhaps, rather than parking the car and then walking, we should try driving down some of the broader paths; we'd cover more ground that way."

Maggie once more studied the maps they'd been given by the tourist board. "So, we're looking for a broad track, one wide enough for a car. They'd want to veer off as soon as possible if we're right, so perhaps, the northern part of the forest would be a good bet. It's one of the few areas we haven't tried."

Nicholas agreed. "We need to try and put ourselves in their shoes—if they wanted to hide, they wouldn't go down the obvious routes. They might skirt off down less-frequented parts of the forest. It's very much hit and miss, of course, as it has been over the last week or so, but we'll just take the first likely looking road which has suitable tracks leading off it."

After cruising around within the forest for a couple of hours along one track after another, they headed off down yet another rutted path and arrived at a spinney with several more broad, grassy tracks leading from it.

"We seem to be going round and round in circles and not doing any better than before. I'm going to suggest that we now get out of the car and split up," said Maggie firmly. "As this is our last visit, we said that we wanted to cover as much ground as we can. It just makes sense this way, rather than driving round and round aimlessly."

She could see Nicholas was not at all happy with this idea. "I'm not having you wandering around on your own. I'm responsible for you if anything were to happen to you. You might get lost. It's just not a good idea."

Maggie felt a familiar stirring of anger. Why did he have to be so autocratic? "I'm old enough to look after myself, thank you very much," she retorted. "I've got a map, too, so I'm hardly likely to get lost any more than you. We'll meet back here in a couple of hours." And with that, she set off and soon vanished from sight.

Nicholas stared after her disappearing figure with a mixture of love and exasperation. He felt a sense of unease, too, and felt half inclined to go after her. "Blast the woman," he muttered as he stomped off in the opposite direction. "Why does she have to be so damned independent? Well, if she gets herself into trouble, she'll only have herself to blame."

After only an hour, however, with nothing to show for his efforts, he decided to retrace his steps. He couldn't rid himself of the niggling feeling that Maggie was walking into some sort of danger.

"I shouldn't have let her go off like that," he said aloud. "My wretched pride! Why didn't I go after her?"

He was about halfway back to the car, when ringing through the forest he heard the sound of a gunshot, rapidly followed in quick succession by two more. His heart seemed to stop.

Chapter 30

Initially, Maggie felt happy with her decision to go it alone. *For once, I've overridden him*, she thought, *done my own thing*, and she wandered down the track she'd chosen in quite a carefree mood.

But after a while, the loneliness of the spot became rather oppressive, and she couldn't help admitting to herself that she would have been glad to see him emerging through the trees after all. It was gloomy without the bright sunshine of the day before, and there was a persistent drizzle that made her feel unpleasantly damp. It was also rather creepy with movements and rustles in the undergrowth as if someone was following her.

"Probably a rabbit or something," said Maggie aloud, trying to reassure herself and hoping a wild boar wouldn't come rushing out.

All this was forgotten, though, when she rounded a sharp bend in the track and as she drew nearer, she spotted some charred pieces of wood at the base of a tree with a scorched and scarred trunk. At first sight, it looked as if someone had lit a fire, but her pulse quickened as she carefully inspected the area around the tree. She found a long stick and started prodding and poking in the undergrowth. She pushed aside some of the brambles and half fell into a depression in the ground. Her foot caught on something more solid, and she realised with a feeling of triumph that she had found part of the metal frame that almost certainly belonged to a car.

With growing excitement and heedless of scratches to her hands and arms, she pushed aside as much of the grass and brambles as she could. In front of her lay the remains of a burnt-out car. There was no sign of bodies, but they would have burnt completely she thought and could not repress a shudder. An unexpected ray of sunlight lit up the area, and she saw something gleaming amongst the wreckage. She stooped and picked it up—it was twisted and tarnished, but unmistakably a gold ring. Could this have been Heike's wedding ring? She wondered. She examined it for a moment and then thought, *I must get back to Nicholas and tell him.*

As she turned to retrace her steps, a twig snapped on the other side of the clearing. Maggie froze. The wood seemed unnaturally quiet, and there was an unmistakable air of menace. Then she saw him—a tall figure standing dark and motionless in the shadow of the trees, pointing a gun straight at her. Maggie's throat constricted with fear, and her eyes widened in horror as a woman appeared beside him. She could only stare in disbelief as she realised who his companion was

'Marta!" she gasped. "I can't believe it. How did you know I was here, and who's he?"

Marta answered calmly enough, though she did not meet Maggie's accusing gaze. "This is Axel. We've been tracking you ever since you left Jena. We knew you'd come here after your chat with Lotte—you should've taken my advice and gone back to Oxford."

Maggie's eyes widened as she recognised the name. "But why have you linked up with him? I thought we were friends." Her voice trembled a little.

' Shall I tell her, or will you, Marta?" drawled Axel, his eyes cold and contemptuous. "She had no choice, my dear. She has a really murky past, this so-called friend of yours. She exposed over half of her colleagues at the university to the Stasi, and as some of them died under torture, she certainly doesn't want that coming out." He openly sneered at Marta. "She didn't take much persuading to keep me up to date with all the information on your poking and prying."

"Blackmail, you mean," snapped Marta, her face white and her eyes full of hatred.

He shrugged carelessly. "Whatever. You couldn't seem to make up your mind which side you were on."

Marta flushed. "You can sneer at me as much as you like. You know very well why I had to work for the Stasi. I had no choice. Anyway, I was only doing low-level surveillance and was just told to keep an eye on your group. In fact, I had a lot of sympathy with Lotte and some of her ideals. I wanted Gorbachev killed as much as she did. He wasn't doing any good for our country."

Maggie gasped, horrified. "How could you? Gorbachev was a really good man.'

Axel spat contemptuously on the ground. "Good eh," he snapped. "Remember Chernobyl? All those denials about what really happened? My brother was sent in there at the beginning to help clean up. His death came

174

slowly, not with a quick bullet. Anyway, I've wasted enough time here. It's time to put an end to all of this and get rid of you, you little meddler."

As his hand tightened on the gun, Maggie, her throat constricted with fear, interrupted him, playing for time and hoping against hope that Nicholas might arrive and somehow overpower him. "Wait," she croaked desperately, "there's something I have to know. Why was Heike involved in all this?"

Axel glanced at Marta. "I think this is your story, my dear," he said silkily.

Marta looked defiantly at Maggie. "That gullible little fool thought she was going to present some petition or other to Gorbachev—she was expendable—we used her to take the heat away from the others. My cousin was riding one of the motorbikes protecting Gorbachev's car, and he pointed out Heike with her petition. Axel was ready to shoot Gorbachev as he got out of the car and came towards her. He was then going to push his gun into Heike's hand and escape with the others during the confusion. But she, the little fool, tried to stop him and got shot in the process."

"So, you lied to me then when you said you were sorry about Heike. I'm now expendable like her, am I?" said Maggie her voice shaking. Marta shrugged her shoulders without looking at Maggie. "Well, at least you can tell me what happened to Heike."

"You'd better ask Axel," retorted Marta. "I wasn't there. It had nothing to do with me." She started to turn away.

"Oh no, you don't. You're not going anywhere. You know too much," said Axel, grabbing her by the arm and pushing her roughly towards Maggie. "You stay there, the pair of you."

Marta, her eyes startled and terrified, tried to protest. He waved his gun threateningly. "Shut up," he snarled at her.

Keeping the gun aimed directly at Marta and Maggie, he skilfully extracted a cigarette and lit it with his other hand, his eyes never wavering. The two women moved instinctively closer together, as if seeking mutual support.

"It doesn't matter what you know now, as neither of you will be around much longer," continued Axel, blowing circles of smoke into the air. He smirked as Marta gave a whimper of fear.

He's enjoying this, thought Maggie. *He's like a spider with its prey—he knows we can't escape.*

"The silly cow tried to stop me firing the gun and got the bullet instead—we dumped her here, and I put a bullet in her to make sure. We'd have buried her to get rid of the evidence, but we got interrupted. The rest you've obviously worked out for yourself," and he gesticulated towards the burnt-out wreckage.

"What harm is there in our knowing all this now?" interrupted Maggie. "You might just as well let us go."

Axel lit another cigarette. "No chance. I've been told to wind this operation up once and for all and tidy up all the loose ends."

"Told? By whom?" inquired Marta, who had recovered some of her composure by now. "I thought you were in charge our end."

Axel glanced at her briefly, "You're not the only one to have a foot in two camps, Marta. I was put in charge of a Chinese cell—backed at the highest level." He looked at the two women, enjoying their amazed expressions. "After that fool Gorbachev stopped supporting the strong Communist government we all needed in our fight against Fascism and Capitalism, Deng Xiaoping was facing pressure for political change. Gorby, who never knew how to stop meddling in other people's affairs then paid a visit to Beijing. He stirred up all the dissidents—they occupied Tianammen Square and, quite rightly, Deng had to crack down."

Maggie couldn't restrain herself. "You mean he ordered hundreds of innocent students to be mown down by army tanks."

Keeping the gun steady, Axel shrugged his shoulders and leant against a nearby tree. "So what—they deserved it. Deng couldn't have his authority shaken up by those unthinking fools—and that's where we came in. Mielke and Honecker needed all the help they could get."

Marta's face was deathly white. "You tricked me, you rat! You always said you were supporting reform. Freedom without social justice is no freedom at all. Those ossified old men were pushing us into civil war."

"You're even stupider than I thought you were if you believed that." Axel's pale eyes were cold and contemptuous. "With Chinese support and tanks in the streets, we could've crushed all resistance—a strong crackdown was all that was required."

"You're insane! You'd have been prepared to see East Germans crushed like insects just like the Chinese in Tianammen Square?" Marta was almost speechless with anger and despair.

"Why not?" Axel threw away his cigarette. He was openly sneering at their incredulity. "We would have been the last bastion of true communism in Europe."

"In which case, you fooled us all, even Lotte." Marta was almost in tears.

He interrupted her. "My, you are a little idealist deep down, aren't you, Marta? What a tiresome person you are. Sentimental enough to hand over Heike's diary too. Emotionalism was always your besetting sin, my dear Marta. You've caused me no end of trouble. Sergei had to be drafted in to get it back. And as for Lotte, that silly old woman—I've already had to have words with her. She's outlived her usefulness just as you have. When I've finished with both of you, I'll be polishing her off too."

His cold gaze shifted to Maggie. "Unfortunately, Sergei wasn't as successful with engineering your little accidents. It's now up to me to finish the job and tie up the loose ends." He straightened up. "You'd better say your prayers. I've wasted enough time here."

He raised his gun, and as his finger tightened on the trigger, Marta leapt forward, her face contorted with fury. The bullet intended for Maggie caught her straight between the eyes, and she swayed and crashed to the ground. Axel muttered an oath as he stared down at her lifeless body. Maggie remained rooted to the spot in horror. Looking at the merciless face in front of her, she realised that she had only seconds to live. Axel took aim again and pulled the trigger. Instantaneously, a shot rang out from the trees behind him. His arm jerked up as he fell into a crumpled heap, blood spurting from his neck. The bullet intended for Maggie's heart grazed her left shoulder, and she, too, sank to the ground with a cry of pain.

Some distance away, Nicholas, who by now was close to where they had left the car, remained motionless for a second after hearing the gunshots. His throat was constricted with fear, and his heart was pounding as he frantically sprinted through the trees in what he hoped was the right direction. "Dear God, don't let me lose her, too! I should never have let her go off on her own. I'm responsible." These thoughts whirled round and round in his mind as he crashed through the undergrowth, his hands scratched and torn, heedless of the branches and brambles in his path. When he finally reached the clearing, his heart stopped as he saw Maggie lying on the ground. He covered the distance between them in two strides and gathered her into his arms, feeling the sticky wetness of blood. "Oh Maggie, Maggie, my darling," he said brokenly. "This is all my fault."

He suddenly became aware of the other two bodies lying on the ground. Startled by the sound of footsteps, he glanced up and saw a woman approaching him, a small silver pistol still in her grasp.

"You," he said accusingly. "If you've killed her, I'll strangle you with my own bare hands." His voice trailed off as he looked at Maggie.

Jutta stared down at him. "You needn't worry, Nicholas," she said dryly, "it's only a surface wound. She's just fainted from the shock. She's got me to thank that she's still alive. Axel would have finished her off as he did Marta if I hadn't got him first." She gesticulated towards Axel's body. "You should reserve your anger for him—he killed your wife."

Nicholas gazed at her in stunned silence.

"He deserved to die," continued Jutta. "He was a pathological killer—absolute scum. He left my sister to burn to death and saved himself. I've wanted to kill him for ages for that, but he went to ground. I promised Lotte I'd do it when she told me he was coming here."

"Have you all been spying on us?" Nicholas was incredulous. "We would surely have spotted the three of you."

Jutta's lips compressed into a thin, humourless smile. "I think you've lost your touch, Nicholas. It's all that soft, easy life in Oxford. You left quite a trail for Axel and Marta to follow, and I was simply keeping tabs on Axel after I'd been tipped off about his movements."

She looked down at Nicholas, who was cradling Maggie lovingly in his arms. She reflected how easy it would be at this moment to kill this man who had caused her so much pain for so many years. Seeing him there, so obviously in love with yet another woman, reminded her of the time she had seen him kissing Heike those many years ago. As she thought bitterly of how she had wasted her youth on this pointless longing for Nicholas and of the lonely years that lay ahead, her heart filled with a burning hatred and despair. Why should this woman have him if she couldn't? Her finger tightened on the trigger. Just one bullet was all it would take. Nicholas raised his head as if reading her thoughts and he looked calmly into her face, his arms closing more protectively around Maggie.

No, Jutta thought, *it wouldn't solve anything. The pain would still be there.* She thrust the little silver pistol into her pocket, turned on her heels and walked away through the trees.

As Nicholas watched her disappear, he felt a great weight fall from his shoulders, and a sense of freedom and joy that he had not experienced for many years. He realised that he was no longer consumed by the overwhelming guilt that had been so much a part of his life. A deep contentment and a sense of being at peace with himself filled him with an inner glow. It was Maggie who had helped bring about this change in him. He gazed down at her face and knew a whole new life was opening up for them both.

Maggie finally opened her eyes and smiled up at him questioningly. "You did get here," she said, her voice trembling. "I've got so much to tell you. What happened? Is everything alright?"

Nicholas helped her gently to her feet. "Yes, Maggie darling, everything is absolutely perfect."

Epilogue

Jutta never came back to England. Julia Streeten received a strange telephone call from her two weeks after Nicholas and Maggie returned to Oxford. She wished Julia all the best and then rang off before her friend could question her further. A week later, the university authorities received news from the police in Berlin that the woman's body found in the Grunewald was believed to be that of Jutta Volk, one of their staff. She had taken her own life. The case was now closed.